Between STEEL AND SECRETS

WILLOW FOX

Published by Slow Burn Publishing

Cover Design by GetCovers

Edited by Marla VanHoy

Proofread by Mikayla R., Ami K., and Jen S.

ONE

HARPER

Stepping inside a police station in Breckenridge wasn't what I had planned for today. But plans change, especially when evidence finds its way into my hands.

That evidence: a stuffed dragon that's been torn and stabbed with some type of weapon, likely a knife.

While it's identical to Zeke's favorite stuffed toy, there's some solace in knowing it's not his.

The male officer behind the desk is in his mid-fifties. His eyes meet Zeke's, and he gives a warm, friendly smile to my son. He offers me a polite nod. "Can I help you?"

"I'm here to report a kidnapping."

He glances at my son.

"Not him. He's mine. This is about another little boy, Rylan Matthews."

His eyes widen slightly.

That name hasn't been on the news in months, but it made a lot of headlines when he and his family were presumed deceased after an explosion.

"Have a seat. Someone will be out with you shortly."

Five minutes turns to ten, and a gentleman in black slacks and a white dress shirt approaches us. "I'm sorry, I didn't get your name."

"I'm honestly hesitant to give it," I say, glancing the man over.

"Zeke." My little one smiles, offering up his name.

Well, shit.

Bringing Zeke may not have been the best plan. The kid might actually tell everyone what I did. And that's assuming I go back home. Well, to the Ricci's home.

My stomach tumbles.

If I don't go home, Luca will be concerned, and since I have his car...

"I'm not sure I thought all this through." I stand, and the gentleman offers me a warm smile. He puts a reassuring hand on my arm. "How about we walk and talk? There's a play area that we could let Zeke explore, and we can sit and chat for a few minutes."

Sighing, I nod. "Okay, yeah."

He ushers me back through the bullpen and to the right, into a small area with a child-sized table and chairs, along with two stacks of toys against the wall.

Zeke eagerly goes to explore while the man gestures for me to take a seat on one of the adult chairs nearby.

"I'm Detective Morales," he says.

I force a smile. "This isn't easy, me coming to you."

"I'm sure." The detective smiles warmly and holds up a finger as he grabs a pen and a notepad from a nearby desk. "You mentioned the name Rylan Matthews earlier, to our officer at the front desk. Rylan is the little boy who died in the house explosion back last winter. But you don't believe he's dead. You mentioned a kidnapping."

I show the detective the gray dragon I had been clutching under my arm. It wasn't entirely hidden from sight, but he glances it over curiously.

"This may have belonged to the little boy. I saw him, the night before the explosion. He was being held by some very ... dangerous men. The mafia."

His gaze tightens as he glances at me then the stuffed animal. He closes the notebook and grimaces. "Did you know the Matthews family personally?"

"No," I whisper, frowning.

"The little boy, his family, their remains were all found in the fire. Unless you have actual evidence that the child is alive..." his voice trails off.

"This belonged to him. I'm sure of it." I show him the dragon again. "Why else would a grown man keep it in his office?"

He's silent, glancing at the stuffed dragon, unconvinced. He shifts in his seat. "What can you tell me about this mafia family that you spoke of earlier?"

Exhaling heavily, I bite down on my bottom lip. "The don is Dante Ricci."

Morales' gaze tightens and his face goes numb.

He's heard the name before. There's definite recognition that flashes across his features.

"How do you know Mr. Ricci?" the detective asks.

My gaze turns to my son. "Does it matter?" I rub the back of my neck, my skin prickling like tiny needles, anxiety creeping over me.

"Go home. Forget you ever met or heard of this Dante character and leave well enough alone. Men like him are dangerous."

"Great," I mutter, standing and taking the stuffed dragon with me. "Tell me something I don't know. Come on, buddy." I hurry over to Zeke and take his hand, letting him know it's time to go.

On my way out of the police station, I head toward Luca's car, when a woman comes barreling outside. "Miss!" She chases after me, slightly out of breath.

Did I leave something behind? I glance back at her as I'm putting Zeke into his car seat. I manage to buckle him in without much protest.

The brunette is about my age, maybe a few years older, wearing a pencil skirt and blouse. Running in that outfit and those heels takes courage and stamina. I turn around to face her, but my back is to Zeke, keeping myself between him and the stranger.

She hands me a business card. "I didn't mean to eavesdrop. I overheard you mention the Riccis, and it's not exactly a secret who they are if you've lived in Breckenridge your entire life."

I glance at the name on the card: *Eagle Tactical.*

"Eagle Tactical?" I repeat, unfamiliar with the company.

"My father runs a private investigation service in town. They do all sorts of private security work, but they're your best bet. I can assure you they aren't lining their pockets with Don Dante's money. You might consider reaching out to them."

I press my lips together and pocket the card. "Thank you, ma'am."

Her blue eyes shine and she laughs. "Ma'am?" Her nose crinkles. "I'm not anywhere near thirty yet!"

Embarrassment floods my cheeks.

"I'm Izzie, by the way." She holds out her hand to properly introduce herself.

"Harper." I take her hand and give it a firm shake. "Thank you for the business card. I'll reach out to your father."

Izzie smiles. "Stay safe. You and your little boy."

"Mama, I'm bored." Zeke kicks his legs from inside the car seat. At least I managed to get him buckled this time.

He's stolen my attention, and I lean in, planting him with kisses before I shut the back door.

"Thank you again." I turn back, and Izzie is already gone, wandering to her blue sedan a few spaces over in the lot.

I take Zeke to the park, as promised, and then grab ice cream for him on the way back. I hide the stuffed dragon under the front seat in the car. Hopefully, no one goes looking for it.

Heading back to Dante's isn't exactly sitting right with me, but I can't not show up; Luca will be worried.

As I approach the main entrance, there is a guard standing at the security post. Recognizing me, he opens the gate and allows us inside. I've seen him a few times wandering the property, but I don't exactly know his name.

There are a lot of Dante's men who roam the property, most of them familiar only at a glance. I couldn't name all the men who work for him.

Parking the car where I borrowed it, I step out and open the back door, helping Zeke out of his car seat.

The front door flings open, and I glance up to see Dante storming outside.

His face is red, his brow furrowed. His posture and the way he holds himself, he's definitely pissed.

"Search the car!" he commands his men.

Two men follow behind him and open the passenger door.

"What are you looking for?" I ask, helping Zeke from the backseat and carrying him inside. He's messy from the chocolate ice cream cone, and he looks to be wearing more than he ate.

Dante's gaze tightens on me.

He doesn't answer.

"We went to the park and to get ice cream."

"You didn't stop anyplace else on the way?" Dante's tone drips with venom, and I try not to let my breath shake.

Zeke starts making siren sounds with his mouth.

Dante raises an eyebrow. "What's that, Zeke?"

His siren sounds grow louder. "We saw police cars."

I force a smile. "Yes, that's right. There were police cars on the way." I'm hoping I can steer this conversation away from our little detour that we made. "Is Luca back yet?"

"They're dealing with some business. They'll be home soon, I'm sure." Dante's eyes tighten, and he glances past me to his men.

"Found it!" One of the men retrieves the stuffed dragon beneath the seat. He lifts it, showing the damaged toy to Dante.

"Mine!" Zeke shrieks. "Give me. Give me. My dragon." His eyes water when he sees the dragon's head bob forward, nearly decapitated.

I ignore Dante and stalk past him for the dragon, its head now ripped even more than it had been earlier. "Look what your men did to Zeke's toy!" I yank it from the taller man's grasp as he stares at me, dumbfounded.

"Sir?" The soldier glances from Dante to me.

I ignore both of them, storming into the house with the stuffed dragon.

Zeke is on full-melt down mode, screaming and crying about his favorite toy. My son doesn't have any idea this isn't *his* dragon, and I can't exactly soothe and comfort him if I want to keep out of hot water.

I'm a terrible mother.

"Tell me you have a sewing kit?" I bark at Dante.

He stares at me, taken aback by my boldness.

Yes, I stole the fucking toy and am now pretending it was Zeke's all along.

I'm not a fucking saint.

Zeke seems to believe it was his, so I have one point in my favor.

Although using Zeke is a shitty thing to do, I'm well aware; but this is the mafia, and I'm not about to get myself murdered or thrown into that basement prison.

Nova comes around the corner, frowning when she hears all the excitement. She glances at the stuffed dragon. "What happened to Zeke's favorite stuffy?"

Thankfully, she's unaware of the duplicate as well.

"Ask that monster!" I point at the man who retrieved it. "He tore its head off."

Zeke shrieks more. The crocodile tears are real, and my heart breaks because he doesn't realize his favorite toy is safely at home in his bed.

"What the hell is wrong with you, Simone?" Nova glares, storming up to him. "What kind of sick fuck likes to make little kids cry?"

He bites his tongue and glances at Dante. "I swear I didn't mean to destroy the stuffed animal. I just reached for it; maybe it got caught on something under the seat when I pulled it out."

Dante rolls his eyes and storms down the hallway to

his office, slamming the door shut. The walls rattle, and I can finally breathe again.

I carry Zeke to the playroom, doing my best to settle him down, but the best distraction seems to be the toys.

His face is still splotchy, his eyes glassy, and he sniffles from the stuffy nose he has from crying, but he's settling down.

TWO

LUCA

The gunfire above has silenced, and I can't help but wonder who won the fight and who lost.

If it's Massimo's men, I'll be dead in a matter of seconds, maybe minutes if I'm unlucky enough to suffer at their hands.

I'm careful not to alert anyone I'm alive until I know which side won.

Massimo grunts beneath me. His face is battered, his body pummeled, but he's still alive, for now.

"Luca!" Ashton's voice echoes in the distance.

My best friend is still alive.

Nova would kill me if anything happened to Ashton.

"Down here!" I shout. "I've got Massimo!" He's pinned under me, my weight pressing him into the earth, keeping him from bolting.

"Like hell you do." He grunts and pushes me forcefully off him.

I go stumbling backward, smacking my ribs into a rock.

"Fucking asshole!" I shout and ignore the searing pain as I throw myself at him and catch a glimpse of the gun in his hand.

We wrestle with the metal, and he discharges the gun into the forest. I knock it several feet away and grab a nearby rock, smacking him over the scar on his face, where Ashton had previously shot him.

I swear the man is a cat with nine lives.

Not if I have anything to say about it.

The trauma to his head knocks him unconscious.

He's still breathing, for now.

Blood drips down his eyes and across his cheek.

Catching my breath after the jolt of pain to my chest, Ashton finally makes it down the mountainside. "Is he still alive?" Ashton nods toward Massimo, whom I have pinned beneath me once again.

I'm not taking any chances.

"He's got a pulse."

"Luca, you down there?" Halsey shouts at us.

"Yeah! I've got Massimo pinned and unconscious."

"What the hell are you waiting for? Finish the job!" Halsey's voice echoes through the forest.

I glance at Ashton. "That would be murder."

I've never killed anyone in my life.

"Do you think he's going to stop coming after your family?" Ashton snaps at me.

He's right.

Massimo doesn't make empty threats.

My mouth is dry, and I want to kill the man who has been threatening my family, but how will I know the threats end with him?

Footsteps crunch over dried leaves and branches.

Halsey slides a few feet down the mountainside until he comes to tower above me with Ashton at his side.

"What are you waiting for? He threatened your wife and your son." Halsey's eyes tighten. "He kidnapped those children!" he shouts and points up toward the top of the ridge where this all began.

I grab the gun from Ashton. It's the only way to know Harper and Zeke are safe—*my wife and son*.

Heat and anger surge through me as I unload the clip.

There's zero chance Massimo survived the stream of bullets to his head.

Halsey smiles.

His sinister grin makes my stomach flip, and I climb off Massimo and hold my stomach.

I will not vomit on the dead body.

Ashton offers me a hand.

I'm covered in blood, it's smeared on my hands, but my shirt is caked in splatter. It's not a great sight.

"We'll dispose of the body," Halsey says. "Ashton,

take Luca back to the compound." He tosses him the car keys.

My mind is in a fog, playing over the events repeatedly. "What about the girls?" My eyes widen in horror. If we did this for Dante so that he could traffic them, I'll kill my father myself.

"We have a contact who can help them."

"Please tell me it isn't the police." Ashton's brow is furrowed.

Is he worried for me because I killed Massimo, the fact that I just used his gun, or for the other men who were killed?

"Of course not. We have a few officers on our payroll, but not to worry. Dante will reach out to our source. He'll get the girls new identities and arrange for their safe travel out of town."

Dante, a good guy?

I'm not sure I believe it.

My head swims as Ashton and I head up the mountain, a difficult terrain to climb, and we reach the awaiting vehicle.

I shut my eyes, trying not to replay Massimo's threats and his death over in my head.

It's a bad movie that I can't erase.

The ride between us is quiet as he takes the wheel, and I eventually stare off into the distance.

My clothes will have to be burned, as will all the other evidence.

Ashton glances at me as we reach the house. "You're one hell of a sight. Try to sneak inside and go shower before anyone notices."

I glance down at my hands. My knuckles are covered in dried blood. My shirt is gross, and I haven't so much as looked at my reflection in the mirror. It can't be good.

Ashton parks in the garage around back, and I hurry in through the side entrance of the house. I leave my shoes by the door, as if that's the worst thing I'm bringing inside.

I have to walk the long corridor to head upstairs to shower.

I try my damndest to be quiet, but Harper somehow catches sight as I walk by the playroom.

"Luca?"

I freeze, doing my best not to move. Worried that if I turn around and face her, she'll see all the crimson staining my skin.

She's swift, jumping the baby gate, which was helpful when Zeke was smaller, but he's learned to climb it by watching Harper.

Hopefully, he won't try that right now.

I hide along the other side of the wall, making her step fully out into the corridor to see me.

Harper's eyes widen, her breath catches in her throat, and she runs her fingers over my cheek and down my chest. "Are you ... hurt?"

"It's not my blood." I shake my head, trying to ease her of any and all concerns.

Her brow is pinched as she stares up into my gaze.

"I'm fine. I just ... let me go shower. We can talk after."

I pull away from her, not wanting her to be covered in Massimo's blood as I retreat for the stairs.

Dante's office door swings open and he steps out, glancing me over. "Luca. After you clean up, I'd like a word."

"Of course." I expected nothing less. I'm sure he wants to be caught up on the situation and the news about Massimo.

I head upstairs for the shower, and now I'm beginning to understand why the floor is marble. Perhaps it's to keep blood from staining it.

I step into the bathroom, grimacing at the splatter of blood covering my cheeks. I strip down. My clothes are going to end up in the trash, no sense in trying to remove the gore caked to the cloth. I turn on the shower and wait for the water to heat before I step under the spray and rinse away the death and filth that covers me.

There's a soft knock on the bathroom door.

"It's occupied!" Does the sound of running water not make it clear that someone is in here already?

A small gust of cold air hits me, and I turn the shower hotter.

"It's me," Harper's voice fills the small space of the bathroom.

"I'll be done soon."

I scrub at the blood that I can see—on my hands, knuckles, beneath my fingernails. I shove my face under the spray and rub at it, hoping to remove any trace remnants down the drain.

"I stole something today."

Harper's soft voice catches me by surprise. I pull back the shower curtain and glance at her. "What'd you steal?" I can't imagine Harper ever doing anything illegal or bad.

She's practically a saint compared to me.

Harper gestures at my face. "You still have some—"

Sighing, I shut the shower curtain and shove my face back under the spray, scrubbing more at my cheeks and nose.

"Do you want my help?"

"I'd love for my wife to join me in the shower, but not when it's a bloodbath in here." I glance down at the floor.

The water is running clear, but just the thought churns my stomach. I still see blood from the splatter of bullets into Massimo.

Harper pulls back the shower curtain, and she's got a white mini washcloth. She douses it under the spray and then reaches up to my face to scrub the last remnants of blood away.

Her touch is warm, strong, comforting.

I'm shocked that she hasn't run away after seeing me covered in blood.

"Do you want to talk about what happened?" She douses the washcloth under the spray again and grazes my cheek with her hand.

"I'd rather talk about what you stole. Was it from my father, or did you leave the house today?"

Harper inhales a breath. "Did Dante speak with you already?"

"No."

What's she talking about?

I inhale sharply, my gaze sharp and threatening. "What'd you steal, Harper?"

"It was nothing. I mean, hardly anything."

"Out with it," I bite, my tone short and clipped. I don't like Harper hiding things from me.

"There was a stuffed animal in your father's office, a dragon. The same one that Zeke has, and it had a gash in its—"

I shut the shower curtain.

"I can't deal with this right now!"

She found the dragon from Massimo. The threat to my family.

Tears burn my eyes.

"Luca," her voice is soft, filled with concern.

"Give me some time to finish my shower. I'll talk to you after. Please." My voice cracks, and I cough to clear my throat, not wanting her to hear the pain in my tone.

Silence fills the space. I turn the shower hotter, letting it scald every inch of me.

Finally, she relents. "Okay. We'll talk after."

The bathroom door opens, and once again another chilly breeze hits me from the air conditioning before I hear the click.

I swear I locked that door, but it wouldn't surprise me if she knew how to pick a bathroom lock.

It's not that difficult.

Finishing my much-needed shower, Ashton offers to discard my clothes, and he bags his own dirty ones from today, letting me know all evidence will be erased.

There was too much evidence today, it's a bit unsettling. But I trust Ashton and I have to trust my father.

I head down to Dante's office. I'm not exactly looking forward to the conversation he wants to have.

Harper came clean, she confessed about stealing the stuffed dragon. I'm not sure why she stole it or what she planned to do with it, but I'll find out eventually.

As it is, she doesn't know about the threat from

Massimo, and seeing as how he's dead, there's no reason to worry her.

It's all in the past.

I head to my father's office. Moreno stands outside the door. "He'll be back in a minute, but go ahead inside. I know that he wanted to talk with you."

I step inside and close the door behind myself.

I'm surprised he wasn't asking to speak with Ashton as well, but perhaps he's got him running other tasks —hence putting our clothes together to burn.

Everyone has their own role, I suppose.

My gaze moves over Dante's desk. There's a stack of papers in the corner and an envelope that remains sealed. The return address is clearly from a bank; that's not the unsettling part. It's who the envelope is addressed to, a PO Box from out of state.

I recognize the name: College Athletics Hockey Foundation.

That's the foundation that granted me a full hockey scholarship.

Why is Dante receiving mail addressed to them?

I grab his letter opener and tear the envelope open in one smooth motion, retrieving the letter.

The office door squeaks open, and I don't so much as blink. "Why do you have a bank statement for the College Athletics Hockey Foundation?" I glare at Dante, demanding to know what he's gotten himself involved in.

My father hates hockey.

He hates even more so that I play hockey.

"Why don't we first discuss your wife?" Dante gestures for me to take a seat in the chair opposite his desk.

"Harper told me she found the stuffed dragon. What the hell were you doing bringing it up out of the basement? Zeke could have seen it!"

Dante clears his throat. "He did see it, thanks to your wife sneaking into my office and stealing from me."

I toss the bank statement across the desk at him as he takes his seat, expecting me to do the same. "Now, you explain the scholarship foundation. Are you behind it?"

He strokes his jaw, silent.

"Well?"

Why can't he just answer me when I ask him a damn question? His silence is guilt. Except the man has not an ounce of remorse in his blood for anything that he's ever done.

"I may have wanted to ensure that your future and mine were protected."

He can't be serious. "What the hell does that mean?" What did he do? My stomach drops to the floor, like being on a rollercoaster heading straight off the track.

"It means that I wanted to make sure the other children of mafia families were around you, protecting you, making you see the light."

I fall back into the chair behind me. "You expected that they'd convince me to join your little crew and become just like you."

Dante smirks, proud of his plan and his accomplishments. "It worked, just not like how I had planned. Consider it an added bonus, me paying for your friends' tuition for four years."

"You're sick."

He clasps his hands together on the desk, watching me intently. "I'm a lot of things, but unwell is not one of them."

I can't even fathom the lengths that Dante went to do this. It stuns me that he would plan so elaborately when he knew how much I despised him. "Do Ashton and Liam know?"

"Their fathers are aware of the circumstances and agreed, considering my investment in their children's futures. Besides, it ensures they, too, join the family business. Ashton works for me, which is pleasing his father greatly."

"And Liam?" I hadn't been aware he had been on a scholarship. He'd never mentioned it to me. He also avoided any topic in dealing with our parents, which made me unsure whether he loved them or resented them for his upbringing.

"Liam and his sister were both offered the same opportunity. Only one of them chose to accept admittance to Evergreen University."

"Does Liam work for you, too?" I'd never seen him at my parents' house, but that didn't mean he may not have had orders to spy on me or Harper.

It was the kind of dirty work my father loved to hire underlings for.

"Whom I employ is none of your concern, Luca." Dante stands and removes his jacket coat, placing it on the back of his chair.

I inhale sharply.

It wasn't an act of denial. Liam may be on Dante's payroll. It's a question I'll have to ask him when I get home.

Liam would be honest with me, wouldn't he?

Although, I can't help but consider that he's been gone a lot and keeping secrets.

He had just been in the emergency room the night prior.

"Liam *does* work for you!"

Dante's gaze flickers for a fraction of a second. I'm unsure if it's because I'm right or he's surprised by my sudden outburst.

His top lip curls up as he speaks, his tone menacing and thick with annoyance. "Quit harping on about your friend! My concern is your wife. Harper is more than an annoyance to me, she's a liability. A problem, son, that you need to handle."

"My wife isn't the problem."

"She is, because if you won't handle her, I will."

"If you so much as harm a hair on her head—" I threaten, standing, snarling, prepared to throw myself across my father's desk and strangle him if need be.

The amused smile lights up Dante's dark features. "I have men for that, boy. Don't you forget."

His condescending tone irks me, but no worse than the next words that pass through his lips.

"I created that marriage of yours, and I can just as quickly snuff it out."

"You've done nothing to help. You wanted Harper to marry Ashton!" The rage burns inside of me, just envisioning the two of them together, blissfully wed. His hands roaming against her body, his mouth on her skin, his lips caressing her—

Heat and nausea overwhelm my senses, and I reach for the letter opener, the sharpest blade on his desk, and grip it like a dagger.

"You have a problem with Harper, you come to me," I grit.

"Put that down before you take out your own eye." Dante smirks, and the smile grates me even further. "I'll have you know your wife tried the same maneuver while you were away, except she had the audacity to put the blade to my throat."

"She should have killed you."

Dante shakes his head, clearly amused. "She wasn't quick enough. The girl doesn't have the reflexes of a natural-born killer. Can't say I'm surprised, since she went to the police this afternoon."

"What?" The blade drops from my hand, clanking onto the desk.

That doesn't sound right.

He's lying.

Why would Harper go to the police?

"I received a phone call this afternoon that a girl matching Harper's description, with a toddler named Zeke, paid a visit to the Breckenridge Police Department. Do you want to interrogate her, or should I?"

My breath catches in my throat, the room spins, and I shake my head.

"I'll take care of it."

"You'd better, or she's going to send your ass straight to prison." Dante glances me over. "Halsey gave me the report on what went down this afternoon. You finishing the job and stopping Massimo, it needed to be done, but Harper, if she so much as comes up with anything tangible to give to the police—"

"She won't," I cut him off.

"You'd better hope not." Dante stands and grabs himself a drink. "Your wife is becoming a liability, and you know what we do about liabilities."

My jaw clenches tight. "Don't threaten my wife." I stalk over as he pours his scotch and swirls it around the glass.

Dante takes a sip, raising an eyebrow. "Let's be honest with one another. You didn't even want to marry the girl. You only did it to spite me."

"In case you forgot, I married her to protect her. You've wanted her dead since thirty seconds after you first met her."

"Not true." Dante tsks. "She shouldn't have gone snooping."

Irritation claws at my skin. I reach for the bottle of scotch, pouring myself a drink. This time, Dante doesn't even bother to object.

Harper has a habit of doing things she shouldn't, and I'm beginning to realize it's probably a bit more than I bargained for when I married her to protect her.

I didn't realize she would constantly be causing more trouble. But she's *my* trouble to deal with, not Dante's.

"I'm not going to apologize for the worry that she's caused. This time or last." I stare at Dante and then glance down at the scotch. The scent burns my nostrils, and I take a sip, doing my best not to grimace.

"Keep her out of my office and away from the police. We don't need local cops or federal agents digging around our home. In fact, I think it'd be wise if you took them home tonight."

I throw back the rest of the scotch and swallow hard. The reason I'd brought her here was to protect her, little good that's done.

"We had an unexpected visitor this morning," I remind Dante. He'd seen the footage on the cameras of one of Massimo's men sneaking around outside. Liam had caught him and disarmed the man before sending him away.

Dante takes a sip and then steps back behind his desk. "I have to protect the family, son. If your wife isn't willing to be a part of the family, then perhaps it's time we cut her loose."

I unintentionally drop the glass I've been holding, and it shatters on the marble. I don't so much as look down at the mess I've made. "Are you done threatening my wife?"

THREE

ASHTON

Protect Luca. That's what Dante instructs me to do, not that I don't already know my job. I gather my clothes and Luca's and take them out back, burning them in a bonfire.

The clothes are the easiest evidence to destroy.

I gave Luca my gun to use to kill Massimo.

There are also the bullets in the other SUVs, not the one that we drove back, which will undoubtedly end up over a cliff somewhere and burned beyond recognition.

That isn't my concern.

"Ashton," Nova's soft voice forces me to turn around, and I glance over my shoulder at her.

"Bonfire tonight?" she asks and raises an eyebrow when she sees that I'm not only burning wood. "Oh."

"You should go back inside."

She huffs under her breath. "Like I'm not aware of the shit that goes down here every single day."

Nova is a bit of a spit-fire. I like that about her. She stands up to her father and isn't afraid to call him out on his crap.

She grabs a nearby lawn chair and slides it over to sit. It's not like she needs to be close, it's still warm this summer evening.

I'm looking forward to winter when I get back on the ice with my friends and teammates. It isn't coming soon enough for me.

"Are you going to stand there or join me?" Nova quips.

I crack a grin and stalk over toward her chair, pretending to sit on her lap.

"Go ahead." She gestures for me to sit with her.

I'm pretty sure I'd crush her if I sat on top of her. "Switch with me," I offer and wait for her to stand before I grab her chair and then pull her onto my lap.

Nova immediately leans back, letting me embrace her as she sits on my lap. "You're not worried about your father seeing us like this?" I ask, my breath tickling her ear as I wrap my arms around her waist.

Her eyes widen and she bolts right off me like lightning just struck.

"Where are you going?" I ask as I watch her dally off from the fire.

"To grab another chair!" She heads across the lawn, grabbing a second chair that was near the back garden before the forest, and drags it with her to sit beside me. "Chair thief." She playfully snarls at me, and I blow her a kiss.

"Don't do that!" Nova holds a finger up at me, warning me to behave.

"Why not?" I'm all smiles. The girl has the ability to make me forget about the exhausting day, the threats, the death, and turmoil.

"My father might see!" Her eyes widen and she glances around outside. It's dark, and unless someone is watching from the window, I doubt the cameras can pick up subtle movements.

"Your father—"

"What?" Nova asks and glances over her shoulder like he's coming.

Except he's not.

Her father knows about us. He's not happy about the arrangement, but he's never threatened me over it. He did, however, try to get me to marry Harper. Perhaps that was his way of trying to break the two of us up?

It seems Nova isn't aware that her father knows about our relationship. We have been mildly keeping it a secret. I haven't screamed from the rooftops that I'm fucking her.

Although, according to Luca, that might not be the case.

"What's so bad about Moreno knowing we're dating?" I ask, curious why she's so gung-ho about him not finding out.

"He works for the mafia!" Nova stares at me, like I should be on the same page as her. Except, I'm not.

"Obviously," I say and smirk. I reach for her hand, missing the close contact. I liked when she was seated on my lap, even if only for a moment.

She squeezes my hand and then pulls apart.

"Come on, what's the worst thing that could happen?" I try not to smile, because the way I see it, Moreno already knows, and Nova is the only one panicking over absolutely nothing.

I scoot her chair closer to me, putting us right next to each other. My fingers move to her thigh, my thumb circling over her skin, inching slightly higher as she squeals and shoves my hand away.

"You're intolerable!" Nova's eyes are like two saucers as she glances around.

"What'd I do?"

"There are cameras everywhere! Don't you value your life?" Nova's voice trembles, and I can't stop myself.

My fingers graze her chin, and I bring her lips to

mine. "Apparently not. I value yours above all else." I lean in and kiss her.

Her body relaxes for a fraction of a second before she slaps me and shoves my hand away. Nova stands and backs away, muttering under her breath that this can't happen here.

"You just hit me." I'm dumbfounded; the sting against my cheek burns and I can't quite ignore it.

It's not like we haven't shacked up together under Moreno's roof, but it was late at night and in my bedroom.

Nova grins and glances away. "I told you no. You should have listened." She saunters off toward the door, and I chase after her.

My arms wrap around her waist, and I spin her around to face me. "You're right. I'll respect your wishes. I won't kiss you," I whisper, my breath teasing her lips apart, but I don't close the gap.

I drop my hands from her hips, and I swear I hear her whimper.

"I won't touch you." I remove my hands from her waist, giving her exactly what she's been asking for.

Nova leans closer to me, I'm not sure she even realizes that she's doing it.

"We won't share a bed tonight," I whisper, and her gaze falls to my lips. "No kisses. No touches. No cuddling together and sharing a blanket. None of it."

She pulls her bottom lip between her teeth. I know the restless and needy look in her eyes, and she's teetering on desire winning, but I won't let it. She's drawn the invisible line, and I won't cross it.

"Good." Nova forces the words out, but I can tell she doesn't mean them. "You hog all the blankets anyway." She snickers, and I refrain from letting my fingers graze her cheek.

"There is something that you should know—"

"What?" She stares at me, waiting for me to answer, hanging onto my every word.

"Your father already knows about us."

Her eyes widen and her face goes ghastly just as her lips part. Had she not made it clear that she wants nothing to do with me tonight, I'd be kissing her right now, reassuring her that everything is fine, but instead, I waltz past her and head inside the house.

"No." Nova's in mere shock, shaking her head, denial setting its course, as she stands there, unmoving. "He can't know."

"He's known for months." Do I tell her about Dante ordering me to marry Harper and wanting to keep it a secret?

"How long?" Nova rubs at her forehead and studies me.

I contemplate how much to tell her. Is it worth her knowing all of it? What good would it do for her to hear how they wanted me to marry another woman? The last thing I want is to upset Nova.

"Don't lie to me, Ashton."

"A while. Before their wedding." I gesture to the house, hoping that answer will suffice. It's the truth, I'm not lying to Nova, but I don't see any point in revealing anything that might upset her. Especially since it doesn't matter anymore.

Harper and Luca are wed.

"And you kept this to yourself?" Nova's eyes widen. "Why didn't you tell me?" She smacks my arm and stomps toward the door of the house.

"For this reason, precisely. I didn't want to get my ass beat by a girl." I'm smiling, and she's glaring at me.

"You're sleeping alone tonight, Ashton."

I was already planning on that when she told me to keep my hands to myself a few minutes ago. "Okay." I try not to feign hurt.

We head inside, and Luca is barreling right at me. "Pack your things, we're leaving for home in ten."

I glance past him in the direction of Dante's office. "Does your father know we're going home?" I would have expected him to encourage our stay, if not extend it. While Massimo is dead, I'm unsure who will take over his position if the threat remains to Luca and his family.

"It was his idea." Luca turns and heads for the playroom.

"Okay." I glance at Nova, who has a frown on her face.

"That feels ... weird. Am I missing something?" Nova stares up at me.

"I think we're both a bit behind on whatever it is that's going on. I'm sure Luca will catch us up on the drive home." I head inside the house and up to the second floor to grab my bag. I carry mine and Nova's down to the car, packing our belongings into the trunk.

Luca is buckling Zeke into his car seat, and he shoots a look at Harper. "You're sitting up front on the way home. You and I need to talk."

"Oh. Okay." Harper purses her lips but doesn't say anything. Wordlessly, she climbs into the passenger side and shuts the door.

I'm grumbling under my breath. I hate sitting in the backseat. Being tall sucks, and there's absolutely no legroom. "Can you scoot the seat a bit forward?" I ask Harper after I climb into the back.

Zeke sits between Nova and me in his car seat, and I'm grateful when Harper slides her seat a few inches forward.

I'm still a bit squished and I shift my legs, using the space in front of Zeke to stretch out. It's not like he needs it.

The minute the doors are shut and we're exiting the property, I can't help but ask, "Do you plan on telling us why we're leaving tonight?"

"Ask my wife," Luca growls and glares at her.

Harper shakes her head. "I don't know." But I sense she's not saying everything.

And as much as I don't want to eavesdrop, it's impossible not to hear their conversation.

"You went to the police station this afternoon, does that ring a bell?" Luca hits the steering wheel, and my eyes widen.

"Ooh shit." What the hell was Harper thinking?

Luca continues speaking, as if my outburst meant nothing. "You forgot to mention that to me when you told me you stole something from Dante. That's the bigger story, Harper!" his voice booms in the small confines of the vehicle, and I glance at Nova.

She shakes her head, clearly surprised to hear the news as well.

It turns out, she wasn't in on whatever Harper had been planning to do.

"What'd she steal?" I ask, leaning forward, deciding that if I have to listen to the two of them fight, I might as well ask the tough questions.

Harper sighs and glances back at me as best she can, turning in her seat. "Dante had the same dragon that Zeke has at home, except its head was shredded. I assume it had belonged to Rylan."

"You assumed wrong!" Luca snaps and he swerves for a moment on the road, putting both of his hands back on the wheel.

"Wait, was the dragon for Zeke?" She pauses and lets the idea simmer in her head. "It was a warning, wasn't it?"

She's figuring it out. I glance at Luca, letting him answer that one.

Luca's jaw is tense and his knuckles are white on the steering wheel. "The man who threatened our son, our family, he's dead."

"Luca," I say, urging him to be quiet. If Harper truly went to the police, then we can't trust her. Confiding in her might get us both thrown in jail. We have to be more careful, keep her out of our business involvement.

"She should hear the truth." Luca shifts in his seat.

"Are you sure you want to risk doing that? She could have a wire on her."

Harper huffs and turns around, glaring at me. "Stay out of this, Ashton!"

"No!" I refuse to back down when she's risking all of our lives. "You think you're so noble, but you don't know what we do, how we just helped dozens of girls being trafficked and sold by a dark and seedy organization."

"You mean your father's business." Harper doesn't sound convinced, and she folds her arms across her chest.

The girl has a bit of a defiant streak. She reminds me a bit of Nova, but my girlfriend is keeping her mouth shut, watching the arguing volley back and forth.

"No." Luca glances at Harper before returning his attention to the road. "My uncle apparently runs his own empire and has been moving girls through town. We rescued them."

She shakes her head in disbelief. "If you did that, why wasn't it on the news? Why did you come home covered in blood? Stop lying to me, Luca. You owe me the truth."

"That's enough!" Luca fumes and shifts again in his seat, his foot heavy on the gas as we cruise closer to campus.

"Uh, Luca, you might want to slow down, we're heading into a residential neighborhood." I can see the speedometer, and he's nearing eighty.

"Fuck." He hits the brakes and glances around, exhaling heavily through his nostrils. "You and me," he glances at Harper, "we'll finish this discussion at home."

Harper glances out the side window. "Fine. Whatever you want, *boss*."

I bite my tongue and then can't keep quiet. Maybe they'll talk at home, but I want to know why the hell she went to the police. What did she tell them?

"We're going to make a quick stop for dinner," Luca says.

There are no objections, and the silence is nearly deafening when we stop inside and grab fast food at a burger joint.

Harper and Luca barely exchange two words to one another. I keep glancing at Nova, who is buried in her chicken sandwich. She's the only one who chose chicken when the restaurant is known for burgers.

The girl always has to be different.

She side-eyes me with a grin, but quietly eats. None of us want to break the spell of silence and have the staff or other patrons overhearing our conversation.

We eat rather quickly, and when we finish, we pile back into the car. Zeke is a bit more fidgety and restless, but I make faces to distract him while Luca buckles him into the car seat.

Once we're back on the road and minutes from home, I can't stand the silence. When we were eating, it was fine. I was hungry, happy to devour my meal in peace and quiet.

But now that we're done, I want answers. I'm sure everyone in the car wants to know what the hell Harper was doing.

I lean forward. "Harper, who'd you talk to at the police station?"

She shifts in her seat and cranks her neck back a bit to eye me. "Does it matter who? Do you know the officers?"

Luca's shoulders stiffen as he drives, but he focuses on the road, at least mostly. The tension hasn't been dispelled. It'll be a while until things are peachy again between those two lovebirds.

Harper grumbles when she finally answers my question. "A detective, but don't worry. He didn't seem particularly interested in looking into anything. Told me to be careful and get out of there."

"And where is the stuffed dragon?" Luca asks.

"Dante has it in his possession..." her voice trails off and she glances at Luca.

"We'll talk later, just the two of us." She agrees, like she just realized something and wants to keep me out of it.

The fuck she will.

What she did involves all of us.

"I shouldn't have gone to the cops," Harper says and glances back at me. There's a sincere frown on her face, etched with worry lines, like she's realizing she may have screwed up.

"You're right, you shouldn't. Because if you go after Dante, you're going after everyone. Including Luca and me. We're just as much as involved as Dante. Do you not realize that?" It's hard not to feel irritated and angry that she would betray not only her husband, but the family.

All that we've done for her, made sure to protect her with the constant threats, and she's going behind our back trying to get us thrown in jail.

How easily what she did gets under my skin, and I shift uncomfortably from the backseat, smacking my closed fist against the back of her chair.

"Ashton!" Luca shouts at me, and the vehicle swerves. "Don't fucking touch my wife."

I didn't lay a finger on her, but he acts like I did, with the venomous look of hatred in his dark gray gaze.

He returns his attention back to the road. "We're nowhere near done, Harper. Ashton is right. We're all equally involved. Going to the police about Dante is putting your family and friends at risk."

Harper's brow tightens, and she shakes her head. "That isn't true. You both have only been working for him for less than a year. Besides, it wasn't like you had much of a choice. You were coerced into working for him."

"I wasn't coerced into anything."

Luca slowly glances over at Harper, his gaze predatory, like he's worried she might actually be working with the police.

"Why are you looking at me like that?" she asks, her voice raising an octave.

If Luca can't trust his wife, then none of us can trust her...

FOUR

LIAM

The front door swings open with full force, and the entire gang comes charging into the house. I'm stretched out on the sofa, staring at my phone.

I keep debating whether I should attempt to reach out to Bristol or leave her be.

The last time I saw her, we were in the emergency room together. She got two liters of saline, which seemed to help, and then I drove her back to the dorms, where she proceeded to tell me that she never wanted to see me again.

Not a huge surprise.

I wasn't exactly expecting a thank you.

There's tension between all of them, and I can't tell who is mad at whom, but something happened.

"You're back early." I glance at Luca, wondering why they're home from his father's house already. I would have expected them to be gone, at minimum, overnight.

Luca's nostrils flare as he storms inside the house. "My wife decided to pay a visit to the *police station*."

Harper scowls, grabs the bag from Luca's hands and carries it off to the bedroom in silence.

"Damn." If I wasn't already seated, I'd be falling into the sofa on that shocker.

She shuts the bedroom door behind herself, and I glance up at Luca. "Are you okay?"

"Not happy right now," he mutters, and Zeke comes to tackle his legs, giggling.

It's like the kid is attempting to cheer him up.

Luca sighs and lifts Zeke, twirling him upside down through the air, listening to his fit of giggles. At least one of us is oblivious to the drama around here.

"I'm going to check on Harper," Nova says, and Luca grabs her arm to stop her.

"Just leave her be. I'll talk to her in a bit. Right now, I need some space before I blow up at her again."

"Tense drive home?" I guess.

My phone buzzes with a text, and I'm shocked by its sender—Kyler Greyson.

> Thanks for keeping me updated last night. I owe you one.

Never thought I'd have a billionaire, former professional hockey player owing me anything. I try not to smile too wide, but I can't help it.

"Booty call?" Ashton quips, seeing me glancing at my phone.

"No. Is the smile that obvious?" I try to wipe it away, but damn, it put me in a good mood.

Wish I could spread the joy around here, because the tension steaming off Luca and Ashton is worse than when they wanted to kill each other a few months ago.

"You're happy. Did you get laid recently?" Ashton quips.

Nova smacks his arm.

"Ow. What was that for?" He shakes his head, staring at her. "Are you still mad at me from earlier?"

"That's a rude question to ask," Nova scolds her boyfriend.

"If I'm mad?"

Nova grumbles and steps closer, staring up at him. "No, if he's had sex recently. You'd be pissed if Liam asked me that question."

"Of course, I would, but that's because the only person fucking you ought to be me."

Nova tries to suppress a smile, but she's failing miserably. It's cute. "That's not happening tonight, at least not with *you*."

Ashton raises an eyebrow. "Who else do you plan on bringing to bed? This guy?" He jabs a thumb in my direction.

Why are they bringing me into their flirty, fighting banter? "Excuse me? I'd rather fuck Bristol than get in between the two of you and whatever it is going on there."

As soon as the words leave my lips, I grimace, realizing the truth.

I've known it for a while, since that stupid kiss.

I'm catching feelings for Bristol Greyson, and as much as I want nothing to do with her, I can't stop thinking about her.

Ashton smiles down at Nova, wrapping his arms around her waist and then immediately dropping his hold.

Their banter is a bit strange tonight, but it's nevertheless amusing to watch. Besides, I'm glad to have Nova around, she keeps Ashton a bit more in line than he otherwise would be.

Nova glances in my direction, raising an eyebrow. "Who's Bristol?"

"No one," I mutter under my breath.

Luca comes to crash next to me on the sofa, bringing Zeke with him. "Is this the girl you spent all day with yesterday? The one that broke your dick and landed you in the emergency room?"

I roll my eyes and turn my phone around so no one else can see the text message that I've been staring at from her father.

"She didn't break my dick because we didn't have sex. We didn't even kiss yesterday."

"Boring!" Nova climbs onto the sofa, squeezing between Luca and me. She winks at Ashton, who is forced to sit on the love seat on the other side of the room.

"It was anything but boring," I admit. Whenever I'm with Bristol, boring does not describe our relationship, which isn't even a relationship. It's not even classifiable as a friendship.

"Are you going to share any other details, or just relive it in your head?" Nova stares at me, and I hope I'm not blushing.

The room is warm, or maybe it's just the fact there's three of us on the sofa.

Zeke climbs across Luca's lap and lands in Nova's arms. Burying his face in her neck, he closes his eyes.

The little guy is getting sleepy but clearly fighting it.

"Liam?" Nova is waiting for me to answer.

"Right, I, uh, saw Bristol yesterday at the coffee shop. The short version is that she came all the way from Great Falls to see me."

Nova's eyes widen. "That's promising."

"Except that we hate each other. Well, she still hates me, probably more than I hate her. Not that I ever liked her—" I shut my eyes and tip my head back on the sofa.

"Right. You have a lot of strong feelings toward a girl you don't like."

"Hate is a strong emotion," I counter. But Nova is right, the feelings are strong between us.

Luca gets up from the sofa and points at the bedroom. "Speaking of hate ... I need to talk to Harper."

Nova and I exchange a laugh. "I don't think you could ever hate Harper." I've seen the looks those two give each other, how they can undress one another solely with their eyes.

I want that kind of relationship, where it's both passionate and filled with trust.

I'm not sure if I could ever trust Bristol; passion, that's something we have a ton of, even though it's more rooted in hatred than romance.

Lust and hate aren't necessarily opposites, though, either.

Fuck, am I lusting after Bristol Greyson?

Zeke climbs down from the sofa and follows after Luca.

"Daddy!" he squeals, running right up from behind, and Luca swoops down, lifting him into the air and letting him fly like an airplane.

Zeke holds his arms out, sailing through the air and giggling the entire time on his way to the bedroom.

Luca finally puts the kid on his hip and then carries him into their bedroom, shutting the door behind himself.

With Harper and Luca out of the room, I have to ask, "What's going on with those two? You guys mentioned a visit to the police station?" I'm still wondering what the fuck happened today. I'm not usually one for gossip, but if it involves two of my best friends, then I want to know everything.

Nova shrugs, and Ashton stands up from across the room and grabs the empty seat on the sofa.

"I'm not entirely sure. She mentioned stealing from Dante the stuffed dragon that Massimo had used to threaten Luca. But she thought it belonged to someone else—"

"Who?" I ask. "Wait, was he the reason we've been keeping an eye on Harper and Zeke?" I'm trying to wrap my head around what's going on. I feel a bit like Harper, kept in the dark.

"Yes."

"And how do the police factor into this?" I glance between Ashton and Nova.

Nova's voice is soft, fueled with concern. "I believe she may have been trying to take down Dante, without realizing all of our involvement."

Ashton glances at Nova, raising an eyebrow.

"I just mean all of us as family. My hands are clean." Nova holds her hands up in the air. "Mostly."

There's a smirk on her face and I roll my eyes and stand, heading toward the fridge. I could use a beer. "Sounds overly dramatic for a Sunday night."

"Tell me about it," Ashton mutters. "Any more trouble today around here? I heard about the guy lurking this morning."

"He did a little more than lurking," I say. I open the fridge, grab a beer and pop off the lid, taking a swig. "But we scared him off. No more trouble, yet. Do you think he was tied to that Massimo fellow?"

"Likely," Ashton says.

We don't have a massive supply of beer, since getting a hold of it can be a bit difficult during the summer. At least during the hockey season, there are seniors who are willing to buy and supply us a case here and there.

Campus is practically dead, but in a little over a week, students will start moving back into the dorms.

Town will once again be bustling.

I'm looking forward to everyone getting together to practice. A few of us still meet up at the gym daily, but it's nice when it's the entire hockey team.

I'm not thrilled that classes will be resuming and my chances of running into Bristol become nonexistent, unless I'm visiting my twin, Sophia, at Great Falls or we're playing against their team, the Predators.

"Hopefully, we didn't cause more trouble today," Ashton grumbles. "We cleaned up some shit, but I can't be certain more problems won't follow."

"Life of the job." I glance back at Harper and Luca's bedroom. "Unless you mean trouble because of that —" I gesture behind me for their door.

"Harper paying a visit to the police puts all of us on notice. We need to be careful." Ashton glances at each of us.

"I'm always careful," Nova says, pulling her legs up on the sofa beside herself as she leans against Ashton.

He wraps an arm around her shoulders and nods. His eyes are heavy, he looks tired but alert.

"Do we need to start worrying about taking shifts, someone staying awake, watching security feeds outside the house?" I know we've already agreed to not let Harper and Zeke be alone.

Ashton sighs and runs his hands along Nova's arms. "I don't think that's necessary yet. We'll know rather quickly whether everything turns to shit or not."

"That's not exactly reassuring," Nova says.

I bring my beer back into the living room and head toward the loveseat across from Ashton and Nova.

"It wasn't meant to be." Ashton pulls Nova onto his lap. "You don't have to worry; we'll keep you safe."

Nova smirks and stretches her legs out on the sofa. "I wasn't worried. I can take care of myself."

I sit and take a swig from my beer. "Do we know anything about the men who were harassing Harper?" I ask.

Ashton nods, his hands caressing Nova's hips, pulling her closer protectively. "Their mafia don is dead. Now, we wait to see what happens."

FIVE

LUCA

I want to talk to Harper in private, but I have Zeke attached to my hip, and it's getting well past his bedtime.

I shove open the bedroom door, glaring at Harper. She's finished unpacking our bag, the empty suitcase open and shoved up against the wall. Seated on the bed, she's got a book in her hands, capturing her attention.

"I'm going to put this little dragon down for the night. Do you want to tuck him in?"

Harper abruptly shuts the book without even glancing at the page.

"I'll put him to bed." Harper stands, without so much as meeting my stare. She holds out her hands to take him from me.

"No bed. Play time." Zeke wiggles in my arms.

"I don't mind getting him ready and tucking him in," I offer. It's as much of a peace offering as I'm going to make because I'm pissed at her betrayal, but I'm not about to take it out on our son.

"He's mine. I'll put him down." She untangles Zeke from my hold and carries him out of the bedroom and into his room.

I bite my tongue, watching her walk away.

That stings.

I give Harper five minutes, enough time to get him changed for bed, before I poke my head into his bedroom. She's getting him settled under the covers for a bedtime story.

He lies back and reaches for his stuffed dragon, gripping it tight in his arms, hugging it to his chest.

I have to walk away.

I need a minute to myself, to keep my head level.

Watching her interaction with Zeke, shouldn't make me want to forgive her for what she did.

She betrayed the family, endangered all of us, including me.

But maybe she doesn't care about me.

Harper married me to protect her son and herself.

Sighing, I head for the kitchen and grab a drink of water.

Liam glances back at me from his position on the loveseat. He stands and joins me in the kitchen, his beer in hand. "Do you want one?"

Ashton and Nova are cuddling on the sofa, whispering and laughing about some joke between just the two of them.

"Thanks, I'm good with just water, for now." I'm not sure how I'll be feeling after Harper and I talk.

"You weren't in there very long with Harper," Liam says, glancing in the direction of Zeke's bedroom.

"We're putting him to bed. I thought it would be a good idea to have the adults talk in private." I don't want Zeke hearing or watching what I intend for Harper after he's in bed.

Liam nods slowly and takes a sip from his beer. "I know things are a bit complicated right now, but I'm sure whatever she did, it wasn't intended to hurt you."

"She went to the police. How could that not hurt me?" I grimace and suck in a sharp breath, biting down on my tongue.

I'm not going to have this conversation with Liam when I need to have it with my wife, the one who betrayed me.

Hearing her side, there's nothing she could say that would make me accept what she did and forgive her.

I glance at my watch, take another sip of water, and then reach for Liam's beer in his hand.

He willingly offers it up, and I take a long swig, hoping the pain will somehow be dulled.

It doesn't help.

And I've emptied his drink.

I place the empty beer bottle in the recycle bin and then stalk toward Zeke's room, glancing in. She's finishing the last page and tucking him into bed.

I wait until she's nearly out of the room before I wander in, give him a hug and a kiss goodnight, and shut the door behind myself.

"Our room, now," I snap at Harper.

Her expression is sullen, and she wordlessly nods, walking into our bedroom.

I shut the door behind her, and while I don't slam it because Zeke is in bed, it's still a bit more forceful than I'd usually close it at this hour.

"You owe me the truth." I stare at her, my back to the door. I fold my arms across my chest and glance her over.

I'm not convinced she isn't wearing a wire, not after her little betrayal this afternoon at the police station.

Fuck me.

"I told you the truth," Harper says, staring at me. She doesn't look away or flinch as I stride across the room and come to stand face-to-face with her, although she's staring up at me, and I'm glaring daggers down at her.

"You told me what you wanted everyone to hear." We weren't alone when she gave me her little version of *the truth.*

"I was doing it to protect you," Harper says, her eyes wide, exasperated as I run my fingers down her bare arms and reach for her hands.

I lift her arms above her head, guiding her shirt up and off her body, tossing it to the floor.

Her gaze tightens with confusion, but she doesn't question what I'm doing.

"Luca," she whispers, staring at me in her bra and pants.

My fingers smooth down her stomach, her skin soft and warm, making this hell of a lot harder than I intended.

I undo the button on her pants and slide them down her hips, my fingers trailing over her skin, teasing her.

Harper sucks in a sharp breath and spreads her legs for me as I help her out of her bottoms.

It takes all of my willpower not to kiss a path back up her thighs or nestle my nose in her panties and lick her through the thin fabric.

Anger seeps through me, but want and desire floods my senses.

"Luca," her voice is soft, warm, easily forgiving, but I can't pretend she didn't hurt me. Betrayal ices my veins as I force myself to fully undress her.

I need to know she's not wearing a wire.

That her betrayal doesn't run so deep as to intentionally hurt me.

Her fingers move to my chest, lifting the hem of my shirt, and I shake my head no, capturing her hands with mine.

This isn't about sex or desire.

I need to know she's faithful to me and only me.

I reach around and pinch the back of her bra clasp, letting the material glide down her arms, revealing her perfect breasts to me.

My tongue darts out to the corner of my lip, wanting to taste her nipples, kiss a path down to the juncture of her thighs, but I refrain from giving her pleasure.

“Luca,” her voice breaks, when she meets my stare and her hands move from my chest to my waist, her fingers snaking into the front of my pants, teasing my waistband.

I let out a hiss, heat flooding my senses.

The woman has the power to bring me down to my knees with just a simple touch.

Fuck.

I hate being weak.

Control. I need to be in command.

I push her hands away, my fingers hooking into the sides of her panties and sliding them down her legs. My nose is just inches from her pussy, and hell, she smells fucking amazing.

I bite down on my tongue to keep from doing something stupid, like giving in to desire.

Temptation is just a breath away, and I pull back, glancing her over, convinced she’s clean and not helping the police. At least not with a wire.

"Now, talk," I demand, folding my arms across my chest, doing everything in my power to keep from falling weak to her body, her charms, the desires that ebb and flow at me.

Harper's brow pinches and she purses her lips, taking a step back. "What was that, Luca?" She fumbles backward another step, and the back of her knees hit the bed. "Were you just searching me for a wire?"

"Figured me out," I huff with indignation, and she covers herself with her hands, moving to the bed, climbing under the covers, hiding her body from me.

"You're just like your father."

I can't tell if her words are meant to burn, but they hurt far less than I imagined. Perhaps she's right, and I'm becoming more like him every day. Working for him is bound to do that to a man, eventually.

"If you're going to the cops, then I can't trust you." I pin her with my stare and climb toward the bed, feeling heat and need inundate my senses.

"I was doing it to protect you!" Harper shouts at me, her eyes cold as ice. "Why do you have to be so damn stubborn, Luca?"

I laugh.

It's dark, throaty, and filled with disappointment.

"Me, stubborn?" She's the fucking stubborn one, running off before the wedding, going to the police trying to destroy my father's business. At every turn, she's causing trouble. "I'm not the fucking problem!"

Harper winces.

I climb atop the mattress, straddling her.

She's buried beneath the blankets and I've trapped her, made her stare at me, feel my weight as I press her into the bed.

"I'm not the problem. Your father is the problem!" Her shouts are no match for me. They come out weak, raspy. She sounds exasperated as my weight crushes her beneath me. Good.

Let her see who has the real power this time.

"You going to the cops is my problem." I find her arms, pinning her down on the bed, restraining her. "Do you know why it's my problem, *princess?*"

Her top lip snarls at my nickname.

I love how much she hates it. It makes me want to call her that a million times over, to stir her up inside.

The war between us is on.

"I'm not your *princess*," Harper bites back. "I'm not your anything if you keep acting like a monster. Get off me." She wrestles under my weight, the blanket inching down from her neck, exposing the rise and fall of her breasts as I pull back just slightly, admiring the flush of her cheeks and how it spills down to her chest.

"See, that's where you have one thing right. I am a monster." I don't deny it any longer.

After what I did to Massimo, I've become the man I swore I'd never be.

Now, all that's left is to embrace the darkness as it devours me.

"Luca." Her voice cracks and I roll away, feeling her pain and anguish as I release my grip on her.

She pulls the blankets tighter and sits up in bed, her back to the wall, her knees pulled toward her chest.

"What the hell was that, Luca?" Her breath is ragged and her question sharp as I push myself to the edge of the bed, my back to her.

"Like you said, I'm becoming my father." I try to hide the anguish in my tone as I stand, my back to her.

"Luca," she sighs and stands.

From behind me, I hear her rummage through the dresser, and I glance over my shoulder as she slips into one of *my* t-shirts that reaches her thighs.

She looks sexy as hell, and I have to stop myself from letting my mind wander to her naked under my shirt.

"I did something unforgiveable today." I won't say it aloud. I can't trust her, not one hundred percent after what she did. For all I know, the room could be bugged. I had foolishly left her alone earlier while I was in the living room.

"What?" Her soft voice tugs at me, and her hand finds mine as she turns me around to face her.

I shake my head, refusing to reveal all of my secrets, especially the ones encased in steel.

I murdered Massimo.

I exhale a heavy breath and stare into her darkened gaze. My fingers reach for her blonde tresses, tangling her hair into a fist, yanking her gaze up to meet mine.

"You went to the police." I can't just forgive and forget.

"It was to protect you," Harper whispers, unable to move from my grasp.

I release my grip, expecting her to run, but she doesn't.

"How does going to the police protect me?" I growl. Has she lost her mind?

"I thought if I had evidence about Rylan's kidnapping, then maybe Dante would be behind bars and you could play hockey. You'd be free from your father."

I laugh darkly and take a step back.

Her suggestion is absurd.

"Dante isn't the villain." I grimace, knowing deep down that he is, but he's not the worst out there. Massimo was far crueler.

"He runs the mafia, Luca!"

"He protected dozens of girls today, teenagers being trafficked and held against their will. Do you still think he's the bad guy?"

"And what did he do with those girls? How did he protect them?" Harper asks the tough questions.

I head for the mattress, sitting at the edge of the bed. "That's above my pay grade." I don't need to know the specifics, but Dante wouldn't take over the operation and continue what Massimo started. He didn't send us there to kidnap the girls and run our own illegal brothel.

"I'm not answering your questions. Unless you intend on working directly for Dante, you're going to have to accept you can't know everything."

Harper comes to stand in front of me, her legs between mine.

She runs her hands through my hair, her fingers soothingly drawing me closer. My heart and body want her, but my head is conflicted.

"I'm not asking to know everything," Harper says, her voice soft, calm, like she's the one who has mastered control. "I'm just asking for your help in taking down your father."

I laugh darkly and pull away from her touch. "I can't do that."

"Why the hell not? You can't honestly believe you're happy working for the devil. You aren't happy working for him, are you?" She raises an eyebrow, skeptical.

Is she interrogating me?

I scoff at her question. "My happiness is the least of your concerns."

"What does that mean?" She pulls back, like I've just set fire to the room.

She ought to run.

"I married you to protect you, Harper. In case you've forgotten."

Her mouth parts and her jaw drops as she steps backward, keeping her distance. "I'm not stupid enough to think you married me for love, but you said ... you told me you loved me. Was that not true?"

I did—I do—love her.

But right now, being in the same room with her is causing me more pain and grief than I ever anticipated.

"Luca?" Her eyes widen and she fumbles backward, bumping into the dresser. She turns away, clearly hurt, and glances down at her feet. "I don't believe you."

"I didn't say anything," I admonish, rising from the bed.

"You didn't have to, your silence is brutal enough. I thought we were becoming something more, but clearly, I was wrong." She spins on her heels and heads for the door.

"Where are you going?" I call out to her.

Her back is to me.

I can't see her face, watch her expression, to try to read what she isn't telling me. The girl has no poker face, everything she feels is easily seen in her eyes, the curve of her lips, her brow line. She's an open book.

Except when her back is to me, her shoulders tense.

"Maybe I should leave."

"What?" That catches me off guard.

Honestly, I was expecting her to bolt into the other room, sleep on the spare bed in Zeke's room. I'm tired of one of us being in there, but it beats what she just suggested. But her body language screams that she means something else ... and that terrifies me.

"You heard me." Harper spins around and meets my stare. "I want a divorce."

SIX

LUCA

She wants a divorce?

There's no smile. No laughter.

She's serious.

Well, tough shit.

"The hell you do. Riccis don't get divorced." I scowl and stride the distance between us, leaving little space. There's not much for her to breathe without the heat of her lips practically on mine.

"Well, maybe I'm not cut out to be a Ricci!" She jabs my chest, her nose twitching.

I grab her wrist, pressing it against my heart. "You'll always be a Ricci. You're married to me, that's for life. If you want protection from my father, then you stay married to me."

Harper stares up at me defiantly. "I'm not afraid of Dante."

I laugh, darkness seeping out of me. "You should be. Hell, *princess*, I'm afraid of him."

She stomps her foot and smacks my chest with her free hand. "Quit calling me that!"

A smile tugs at the corner of my lips. I tilt my head, enjoying that I can rile her up with one simple term of endearment, which she hates.

"I'll quit calling you *princess* when you get it through that thick skull of yours that you're not the one in charge."

Her eyes tighten, and I've definitely said the wrong thing.

She throws her other hand up at my face, but I'm quicker and I grab her wrist before she can land it across my cheek.

"You're so irritating!" She fights my grip on her wrists. I back her up against the door to settle her down.

"Really? Coming from the woman who tried to have me arrested." I stare into her darkened gaze, and she flinches.

"I didn't ... Luca, is that what you honestly think?" Her voice trembles, but it's not from fear. She sighs and loosens her fighting grasp as her hands come to rest against my chest.

Staring at her is like staring into the sun, and it takes everything I have not to look away. The intensity is hot and overwhelming.

"Luca?" she whispers, and her fingers gradually move up to my cheek. But this time, she's much more tender and gentler. I loosen my grip on her wrist as she caresses my face. "The blood from earlier, the fog in your eyes when you came home. Something happened."

My jaw clenches, and my spine tingles. "I'm not discussing any of it with you." I refuse to bring the words to my lips and speak them aloud, that I killed a man.

Flashes of blood still haunt my vision.

I can't help but replay the scene with Massimo over and over again. It's like a bad movie I can't turn off.

"You don't trust me." Her words are sullen and her shoulders sink as she pulls back. Harper nods. "That's fair."

"How can I trust someone who goes behind my back? You should have talked to me before doing something so careless that could hurt all of us." Anger returns, heat scalding my cheeks.

"I came clean to you that I stole the dragon—"

Is she serious? I laugh darkly and pull away from her, untangling and stepping back. This time, I need space.

"You came clean for your own self-preservation, after you stole from Dante and had gone to the police."

She rolls her lips together but doesn't answer.

Harper must know that I'm right because she'd be arguing with me if that weren't the case. I hadn't realized how much my *princess* liked to argue until we were wed, now it's the one thing we're best at.

Sighing, I run a hand through my hair, frustrated.

"You should have come to me!"

She's quiet, her tongue darts out, swiping across her top lip. Her stare won't meet my intense scrutiny. She's studying the mattress, or perhaps the bed linens, anything to keep from looking at me.

When she avoids my heated gaze, I break the distance between us and guide her chin up, forcing her to stare into my eyes.

Her breath catches in her throat, and I exhale loudly, the heat between us malleable. "I'm sorry." Her voice is soft, tentative, hardly the epitome of apologies.

"Don't apologize when you don't mean it." I drop my hand from her chin and glance away.

"I am truly sorry. I wasn't thinking clearly. I saw the dragon; it reminded me of Zeke's, and I made an assumption that it belonged to Rylan. You once mentioned that your father doesn't hurt children, but then he kidnapped that little boy, and I still can't get all of it out of my head. I saw the news report, I know his family was murdered by Dante. It's awful. Your father can't murder someone and just get away with it!"

Harper is rambling and spiraling.

“What did you think would happen when you went to the police? That they’d take the stuffed dragon, run DNA, then come and arrest Dante?”

Her voice breaks. “Maybe.” Uncertainty clearly reaches her brow. “I hadn’t thought it all through,” she whispers. “I assumed they’d be eager to listen and want my help.”

Harper has no idea what damage she’s done. “Do you know what Dante does to those who betray him?”

“Throws them in that prison basement?” Harper guesses, forcing a smile. “You’d set me free, wouldn’t you?”

I tip my head back. Does she think I have control over my father? “You’re lucky he didn’t order his men to kill you when you came back to the compound.”

Harper exhales softly. “I don’t know how he found out. I was careful not to be followed.”

“Dante has men everywhere in the city, including ones who are on his payroll at the police department. You can’t trust anyone, Harper. Do you understand me? You can't go around stealing from Dante or running what you think is evidence to the police station—"

"What I think is evidence..." she repeats slowly and steps away from me. She paces the length of the bedroom. "Luca, how was I to know that it didn't belong to Rylan? Why is my son being threatened?" Her eyes widen and she bumps into the bed, sitting at the edge.

"You don't need to worry anymore, they're dead."

She stares up at me. "If there are threats being made on my son, I ought to know about them!"

I sit beside her on the mattress, trying to keep my cool. "You can't know about every threat. You'd always be worried, Harper. My job is to protect you."

"No, Luca, your job is to go to school. You work part-time for your father."

"Fine, protecting you is an added bonus," I say, trying to make light of the situation.

She doesn't smile. Her eyes are sullen, filled with pain. We've both caused so much heartbreak between us today.

Harper reaches for my hand, intertwining our fingers together. "I want to tell you something, but I don't want you to get mad," she says.

I sigh. It's not great when she's starting a sentence off like that. I'm hesitant to ask, but I go ahead with it anyhow. "What is it?"

"When I was leaving the police station, a woman came up to me and gave me a business card. Her father runs a private investigative firm. She suggested that they might be able to help."

"Help with what, Harper?" I try to keep my temper even, but I'm reeling inside.

She can't leave it alone, can she?

When will she realize that stopping Dante isn't an option? That keeping him in power protects all of us.

"Do you want to work for Dante? Has something changed?" Her gaze bores into mine and I'm forced to look away.

"I'm—" I contemplate how best to answer.

"The truth, Luca. Just give it to me straight."

I lie back on the bed, staring up at the ceiling, my legs dangling off the side of the mattress. “I love you. I love Zeke. I want to keep my family safe. Would hockey be my preferred choice out of college? Absolutely, but I’m beginning to realize that I will end up working for Dante and I suppose I’ve made peace with that decision.”

“How?” Harper shifts around on the bed, staring down at me. Her fingers stroke my jaw, and momentarily I close my eyes, leaning into her touch.

It’s hard to stay angry at her when she’s trying to look out for me. Even if it’s in some weird, fucked-up manner. “How have I made peace with it?” I ask, chancing a glance in her direction. I force a smile. “Is there another choice?”

She sighs. “I was hoping so, until Dante caught me.”

She’s referring to her afternoon visit to the police station.

“That isn’t going to fix anything. Putting him behind bars, it jeopardizes all of us, puts us all in danger and could get me tossed in beside him.”

Harper scoots back on the bed, drawing her legs up beside her. Her fingers move from my jaw down my neck. Her touch is warm and soothing, bringing my emotions to a calmer state, the reckless energy seeping out to a stillness.

"How would you end up in jail? What did he make you do?" Harper asks.

I open my mouth, then quickly close it.

I want to trust her, but not with what she did today.

"It's better that you don't know."

"Luca, I can't help you if you're not honest with me." Her eyes plead with me to tell her, but my heart holds back the truth.

I want to lean in and kiss her, but it takes too much energy to sit right now. Lying is more my speed, and I let my eyes drift closed.

She gently nudges my arm. "Stay awake with me."

My eyelids flutter open. "I am." I reach for her hips, pulling her down flush beside me, her face just mere inches from mine as she's curled onto her side.

I lean closer, wanting to forget all of today: the fighting, the death, the bloodshed, those girls. Her proximity is surprisingly calming, even after our argument.

She rests her forehead against mine, the heat of her breath warm against my cheek. “I truly am sorry,” Harper whispers, and her voice breaks.

If she cries, I’ll fall apart.

I wrap both arms around her waist, pulling her against me. My lips crush hers, but it’s not enough.

It’s never enough with Harper.

I always crave more.

Rolling over, my weight above her, my body pushes her down into the mattress, and she wraps her legs around me. The shirt rides up, and I realize how little she’s wearing and how I have too many clothes on between us.

I climb off her, and she whimpers, “Luca?” Worry creases her brow, and I lean down, kissing it away before I lift the hem of my shirt and yank it over my head, tossing it across the room to the floor.

“Oh.” The smile adorns her face when she realizes I’m not leaving.

It's cute and flattering how much she wants me.

Her hands are on my hips, helping me remove my pants and boxers in a matter of seconds.

"Are we ... okay?" she asks, pausing before taking things any farther.

"That depends. Do you plan on going behind my back again?" There's more harshness than intended in my question, but she smiles all the same.

"No. Promise me you'll tell me if we're in danger, though."

If I told her every time there was a threat made on our lives, she'd never want to leave the house. I sigh again.

"Luca."

"Fine," I say, and hope that it doesn't come to pass, that, with Massimo dead, the threats to my family are gone.

There's a fire behind her gaze, and I silence her concerns with a kiss, my mouth crushing hers, our bodies dueling for control.

I pin her beneath me, her hands pressed against the mattress at her sides by her head. My hips grind against hers as she moans.

"You have too many clothes on," I mutter in a frenzied state, the shirt tangled between us, feeling like too much.

I help guide it up and over her body, baring her to me. "Beautiful," I whisper against her ear, my lips teasing the skin as her back arches off the mattress.

Her fingernails drag over my skin, along my back, pulling me closer, marking me. The slight singe of pain feels good against the cool air on my back.

Heat floods between us, like molten lava, as I drag one leg up around my hip, teasing her with my cock at her entrance.

Harper arches off the mattress, her lips fusing with mine, and I'm craving exactly what I need: *her*.

One hand untangles from her wrist, needing to feel with certainty that she's ready for me. My fingers deftly spread her folds and feel wetness seeping out of her.

A smile encompasses my face as I stare down at her, amused. "How long have you been turned on, *sweetheart*?"

She momentarily holds her breath and then expels it.

Was she perhaps worried I was going to call her *princess* again? Maybe I should. I like stoking the fire inside of her, watching her fight me, because deep down, I know that she cares.

She wouldn't fight me if she didn't love me.

"Some secrets are best left kept," she whispers and her nose crinkles. The smile plays on her face, and I catch her lips, needing a taste, hungry entirely for her.

She's mine, and I'm hers.

Yet it never feels like enough.

My gaze tightens, and I grip her wrists, pinning them above her head with one hand, my other hand embracing my cock, teasing her folds and her clit.

Her lips part, head bent back, eyes glazed over.

"Eyes on me, baby," I rasp, and she struggles to open those glorious dark eyes as she bites down on her bottom lip.

It's sexy as hell, and I cover her mouth with mine, pushing my tongue inside.

Harper whimpers as my cock glides across her folds, teasing her, but I don't inch inside of her yet.

I like listening to her, needy and desperate.

It's a fucking turn on that riles me up, knowing she wants me.

"Oh God," she moans and wraps her legs around me, trying to gain leverage as I keep her pinned against the mattress.

"That's not my name, *princess*."

She growls up at me, but there's a playfulness to her anger, which only makes me happier.

The smile grows on my face, and her narrowed gaze is sharp, like daggers, but it doesn't stop me from teasing her.

"You're going to be the death of me," Harper mutters as she grinds her hips upward against mine.

She's trying everything she can to fuck me, but I'm dragging the moment out, testing her limits, seeing how long she can last, until she begs me to please her.

Harper isn't the begging type.

But God help me, when she begs, it makes me weak at the knees, and I'd do anything for her.

Absolutely anything.

My lips caress a trail of kisses and warmth across her jaw, to her neck, and the whimper that falls from her mouth is heavenly.

She hums a soft moan, her body fighting against the restraints of my hand on her arms.

If she demanded that I let her go, I would in a heartbeat.

I have her trust, her heart, every ounce of Harper Ricci is *mine.*

I worship her like the goddess that she is, my mouth licking and sucking the soft, supple skin of her neck as she shifts restlessly beneath my body.

Each movement is like fire, making my cock twitch and my heart leap.

“Keep doing that,” I mumble against her skin as she grinds up against my hips, desperately trying to find more pleasure.

Her head is tipped back, eyes struggling to stay open, and they flutter closed every few seconds. “Fuck, Luca.”

“Not yet, princess.” I chuckle and hear the moan spill from her lips.

“I’m going to fucking end you if you don’t let me come,” she fires at me.

Sweet, vicious torture. The agony is gorgeous, shining across her face. She’s practically glowing. “Is that a threat or a promise?” I smile, releasing my hand on her wrists, unbinding her.

Harper takes the opportunity to forcefully roll me onto my back.

She’s not playing.

And I’m here for it, one hundred percent.

I try not to laugh, but I can't stop myself from smiling. "I'd fucking tie you to the bed post if we had one."

Harper grumbles and shoves my hands above my head. She's hovering over me, not quite touching me, other than the grip on my wrists.

"Remind me to invest in a new bedframe."

She snorts and then scowls down at me. "Don't move."

"Don't move my hands? Or don't move my—" I glance down at my cock, which has a mind of its own.

"You know what I mean, princess," she shoots back at me, and while I should be pissed, I love the fire behind her darkened gaze. It screams she loves me, and fuck if I'm not the luckiest man alive.

"I'll be whatever you want." Grinning, I stare up at her. As long as the nickname doesn't leave the bedroom, there are zero complaints from me.

"Don't move," she warns through a threatening tone, "or I'll walk away."

That makes my stomach flop and my insides tense.

"What?" I croak.

My heart jackhammers in my chest.

She'll walk the fuck away from *me*?

"You heard me." She tightens her gaze and saunters down my body with her hips swaying, and damn, I'm not sure if I should be angry or turned on by her threat.

"If you leave me, I'll chase you to the ends of the earth, *princess*."

Her lips part and she gives me an odd look, her brow netted with confusion. "I meant out of the room. Relax. Don't go all caveman on me." She playfully swats my chest, and I can't stop my hand from grabbing her wrist.

Harper's eyes widen. "What did I say about those hands? Above your head, princess. Unless you want me to call in Ashton to hold them down for you?"

I swallow nervously. "Fuck, no. He doesn't get to see you naked." I'm not keen on him seeing me naked, either, but there's zero chance that anyone else gets to devour Harper's body with their gaze but me.

And I'm not into threesomes with other guys. If Harper wanted to invite Kensley or another girl, then I'd be jumping with joy, but fuck no to the third being a male.

"Then keep your hands on the damn mattress," she grits between clenched teeth.

It's actually quite adorable, but I do as she demands. I stick my tongue out at her playfully, and she leans down, capturing my mouth, sucking on my tongue and grinding her hips against me.

Fuck, that's hot.

My cock throbs against her ministrations, and I want to bury myself deep inside of her.

"You're killing me," I rasp, wanting to roll her around, pin her beneath me, and fuck her.

She chuckles down at me, her hand using my precum as lubricant as she strokes my shaft.

My eyes shut, struggling to focus.

Her hand is incredible, and what I wouldn't give to feel those luscious ruby lips wrapped around my member.

"Tell me what you want," Harper rasps, her eyes dark and fueled with want as her breath grazes the head.

It takes every bit of strength to speak, the words raspy and thick. "Taste me."

Her lips descend on my cock and it's pure heaven. Harper's tongue does glorious things as she brings her mouth deeper, taking me farther in, her head bobbing up and down, and I swear, if she doesn't stop soon, I'll explode.

"Fuck, babe, you keep doing that—"

She pops her mouth off and smirks at me proudly. "You'll come early?"

I growl at her and snap my teeth, pretending to bite.

Harper giggles and climbs back up my body, her hands finding mine still held above my head. "Your turn to dominate me," she whispers, and within seconds, I have her flipped on her back.

"Thank God." I wasn't sure how much more torture I could take before breaking her rules.

I climb down her body, my lips leaving a trail of kisses and playful nibbles as I move across her skin.

Capturing a nipple with my mouth, my tongue teases her flesh as she runs her fingers through my hair.

I descend lower. My lips and breath skate across her stomach, dropping soft butterfly kisses, and she hums softly in the back of her throat, a slight moan, entirely for my ears only.

"I love the sounds you make," I whisper and stare at her, watching her face flush.

Harper glances away.

"Don't ever be embarrassed, everything about you is perfect." I spread her legs farther apart as I settle between them, dragging one thigh up and bending it as I kiss a lazy trail along her bare skin.

She's restless.

Greedy.

Demanding more.

"Luca." Her voice is raspy and thick, fueled by need.

It makes my heart soar. I love how she moans my name, and I haven't even brought her close to the edge yet.

"Do you want more?"

"Yes," Harper rasps.

"Tell me what you want." My breath hovers over her center, teasing her pussy lips but not yet touching them.

Harper whimpers, and I watch as she grows restless on the bed. "Kiss me, here." She brings her hand between her thighs, gently touching her mound, showing me where she wants my lips.

"You want me to taste your pussy?" I rasp, staring at her.

Her mouth parts, and she nods ever so slowly through heavy-lidded eyes.

My breath teases her folds, and I draw my tongue over her lips and let my fingers separate them farther, letting my tongue explore over her labia.

She's restless against the mattress, and I smile, knowing what she wants, what she craves.

I let my tongue circle along the sides of her folds, teasing her, not quite reaching her pearl that she's desiring most of all to be caressed.

"Luca." The way she moans my name, the sounds, the sweet masterpiece goes straight to my cock.

It takes all of my focus and patience to pleasure her without getting distracted. I drag my tongue around, teasing the bead and finally flicking her clit with the lightest of touches as her back arches off the mattress.

I know exactly what she likes.

My mouth devours her, my tongue creating a steady rhythm, keeping the same pace, feeling her body movements and listening to her subtle breaths to distinguish the right harmony.

She's a work of art, and as I compose the masterpiece, she trembles and moans like a sweet symphony. The music, a crescendo growing more intense, and I slip two thick fingers inside, stretching her, teasing her in a come-hither motion.

Her pussy walls clench on my fingers, her insides trembling and her back arching off the mattress as I try to keep her steady, my lips never slowing down or letting up.

"Luca—" Her words are lost on her lips, the closeness obvious from her motions alone, but I keep going, wanting to send her over the edge, take her there and watch her spiral toward oblivion.

Her fingers bunch at the bedsheets and then tangle in my hair. Her nails move to my shoulders, clawing and digging, trembling beneath my lips. I keep the same steady pace, feel the wetness seep and taste the sweet nectar as she moans and chants my name, body trembling and arching from the mattress, unable to hold back any longer.

I continue licking and tasting her with my mouth until her body settles against the bed and I climb up alongside her, watching her eyes lazily open with a smile.

"Hey, handsome." Harper grins through heavy-lidded eyes and leans forward for my fingers, bringing them to her lips, licking herself, and my cock throbs.

"Fuck, that was hot."

She intertwines our fingers together, bringing her hands up and pressing them to the side of the mattress, letting me take the lead. "I'm ready for round two," she says, gasping for breath.

I don't know how she has the stamina or the energy, but I'm the luckiest guy in the world because I get to take her.

She's mine.

I drag my cock along her folds, coated in her wetness, and tease her pussy before slowly thrusting inside of her.

She bends her knees, widening herself to me, and I take the plunge. With eagerness, she moans as I fill her.

"Good girl," I whisper, loving the sounds she makes as I slowly begin to withdraw before thrusting again, harder and deeper.

Her fingernails dig into my backside, pulling me closer as I shift my hips and grind into her.

"For fuck's sake," she moans and her nails drag over my back, clawing at me.

Her pussy walls clench on my cock, and she's already trembling.

I've just gotten started, and she's teetering on the edge.

She wraps her legs around me and then attempts to flip us over, but I've got her pinned down.

She grunts and moans, her body edging near, and I have half a mind to pull her from that cliff, make her drag out the next impending wave.

Her fingers move between us to stroke her clit, and I capture her hand, bringing it back down on the bed. I tsk at her with a wicked grin. "This time, I think you'll wait for me."

Her lips part and she moans in protest. I bite down on her bottom lip, tugging it between my teeth, and her eyes slip closed.

Each thrust grows more intense, fierier. "You feel so fucking perfect," I whisper into her ear and lick behind the lobe as she shudders against me.

Another couple of thrusts, and her pussy walls quiver.

"You're not waiting for me," I fume, and she grips my forearms, a foggy daze over her expression as her eyes flicker open and she stares up at me.

"I ... can't," she whispers, and each breath comes out a soft gasp.

I withdraw completely from inside her and she whimpers. "Luca?" Her eyes open wider and a frown crosses her face. "What's wrong?" Her hand reaches my cheek, stroking my jaw.

"On all fours," I command.

"You better fucking let me come again," she mutters and gets herself in position.

I smack her bottom, and she yelps, glancing at me over her shoulder.

"What the hell was that for?"

Smirking, I rub over the reddened spot I marked on her ass. "Doubting me."

Her brow knits in confusion. "I never doubted—"

She's on all fours, and I find her pussy, wet and waiting. I guide my cock into her pussy from behind, and she exhales a breathy moan as I fill her.

"Fuck, that's good." Harper is on her hands and knees, looking ripe for the taking.

My fingers find her clit, circling the bead, sending her body spasming as she tightens onto my cock with each thrust.

A moan spills past her lips and her hands clench the bed sheets, tangling them in fists. She hangs her head, gasping and panting, her pussy walls clenching and shuddering around my shaft.

"You won't come again," I warn.

"What?" Her voice catches in her throat. "Luca?" She glances at me over her shoulder, pure confusion written across her face.

"Not until you beg me to let you come."

"Fuck." Harper hangs her head and I can only imagine the inner turmoil.

She hates begging.

My fingers itch to please her, wanting to hear her plead with me to give her what she most desires.

She pulls away, my cock slipping out, startling me by her movements. "Harper?"

I reach out, wanting to make sure she's all right, my hand on her hip, tugging her around to face me.

With a quick maneuver, she wrestles me onto my back, guiding my cock right back inside her pussy, and damn, it feels like home.

"You'll do the begging," she smirks, staring down at me with a wicked grin.

Relief floods all of my senses.

"Please, Harper, please fuck me." My attempt at begging isn't intended as mockery, but she rolls her eyes and climbs off my cock. "Fuck," I roared and that elicits the response she was expecting.

Her eyebrow arches, and she straddles me once again but, instead, lets my cock teeter at her opening. "Beg me," she grunts, and it's the sexiest thing I've ever heard in my life.

"Harper, fuck me." Desperation pours from my words, my fingers on her hips, digging into her skin.

She smirks and stares down at me playfully. "You can do better than that."

"Harper Ricci, I'm begging you to fuck me, or I'll flip you on your back and shut you up the only way I know how, with my cock inside your mouth while I come."

Her breath catches in her throat, her eyes widening slightly before she guides her weight down onto my cock.

I buck my hips upward, the sharp contrast hard and swift.

Her hand comes to rest on my shoulders as she rides me. With each thrust, I move my hips with her, building momentum.

I struggle to keep my eyes open, focused entirely on her. "You feel so fucking perfect," I rumble as heat courses through my body, tingling all over.

Warmth spreads through me like a spark igniting, and her insides clench around my cock, making me feel every spasm and shudder trembling through her body.

She keeps the rhythm steady, but I need more.

Her head lolls back and she's close, the flush of her cheeks, the gasp of her breath, I recognize when she's teetering on the edge and I keep the same solid tempo to bring her over the brink.

Her lips part, the moan silent at first, until it rips through her. The undeniable sound epic and glorious as she trembles above me, and just as her orgasm subsides, I quicken the pace, my heart hammering against my chest as I roll us around, pinning her under my weight, my arm nestled around her as I move faster and harder, the pain of today bleeding through as I chase my orgasm.

Ecstasy is just a breath away, nearly impossible to reach, fleeting in sweet agony. Harper captures my mouth, her tongue bringing me back to the present as I tremble in her arms, finally shattering and letting go.

Gasping for air, I roll off Harper, lying on my back, an arm covering my face. The pain comes crashing back, the murder, the senseless threats of violence on my family.

Panting, my heart keeps pounding wildly until I feel her soft fingers caressing my chest and dancing over my arm, guiding her hand into my palm.

Gradually, I slide my arm down away from my face, pulling Harper against me, tucking her head under my chin, not wanting her to see the anguish written across my face.

What I've done still stings and tears at my heart. But Harper doesn't need to know. Finding out that I killed a man, even if he was the devil, will change the way she looks at me.

I can't have that happen.

I won't.

I bury the pain, the sadness, the fear, and channel it into something darker.

I have to protect my family, no matter the cost.

SEVEN

BRISTOL

Sunday is a lazy day after my visit to the emergency room. I avoid the text from my father, and when I get to work; Mom is already at my desk.

"How was your weekend?" Mom asks, looking pointedly at me, like she knows more than she should.

"Fine, Em." I never refer to her as Mom at work. I want to be seen as a professional, and calling one of my superiors "Mom" just seems weird.

"Was it?" There's that look, the one that tells me she knows I'm lying or hiding something. She doesn't wait for me to answer. "A little birdy told me you were in the emergency room this weekend."

"Are you spying on me?" I can't believe her! I drop my purse on the desk and stalk off for the breakroom, hoping that Emerson takes the hint and leaves me alone.

Unfortunately, she doesn't seem to get the message.

"There's no need," Em says, and I know she's trying to be protective as my mother, but it still irks me.

Why is she even here? Can't she go back to New York and work the field office back at home?

"I'm not a little kid. I don't need you and Dad constantly worrying about me." I grab a cup of decaf and spike it with a third of flavored creamer to kill the taste.

It's bad enough that they have been renting a home in the mountains. Dad calls it his vacation home. It's more like a place for them to be near me.

Ever since I started at Great Falls, they seem to spend more time here than New York, but it's also the off-season for hockey.

Em watches but doesn't say anything.

"Who told you I was in the E.R.?" I glare up at Em. "Dad texted me yesterday. How did he know?"

Emerson keeps her mouth shut, but there's a hint of a smile on her lips, like she has a secret of her own.

"Mom!" I stomp my foot, demanding to know how she found out. "Was it someone at the hospital?" I'm well aware of HIPPA and the fact that, legally, they're not allowed to disclose personal information, but Dad is a huge donor, so maybe they look the other way when it comes to legality?

Well, screw them.

"Does it matter who told us?" Em walks me back to my desk, and I take a seat, grumbling the entire time.

I should start filing papers, but instead, I want to throw them at her head and make her clean all of it up.

Emerson shows me her phone, and the forwarded message from my dad.

"Are you fucking kidding me? Liam sent the text?" My jaw drops and the anger I felt earlier is nothing compared to the rage barreling through me right now. “I’m going to kill him!”

“Probably not the best words to say around a bunch of private investigators,” Mom quips.

I roll my eyes. “Well, forget you heard them.” I sip my coffee, but it doesn’t take away the anxiety and irritation creeping all over me.

How dare he!

When I explicitly told him not to contact my father, he went behind my back and did so anyway.

What a pompous jerk!

“Listen, I think it was nice that he took care of you. I didn’t realize you and Liam reconnected.”

I laugh darkly. “He’s an asshole. We didn’t reconnect. He just ... it doesn’t matter.” I refuse to explain myself to Em.

She met Liam when we were kids, after the trouble that followed me in the first grade.

Emerson perches herself on the edge of my desk. “Listen, whatever is going on between you and Liam, that's your business. But if something is happening to you, medically, that becomes my business."

"Why?" I glare at her. "I'm an adult. I can make legal and medical decisions for myself."

"Because your father and I care about you. Yes, you're one hundred percent right, you are an adult, but you're also on our medical insurance. So, if you're making a visit to the emergency room, unless you plan on footing the bill, we're going to know about it, and we're going to ask questions. Besides, if something is wrong, your father and I want you to get the best care."

I snarl at her and push my coffee cup away, no longer interested in it. My stomach is churning and I can't handle another sip of the sweetness this morning.

I get that she's trying to be helpful, but I've always had weird symptoms since puberty. It's just that they've gotten worse recently. The last thing I want is to be pulled out of school right before the semester starts and forced to have a mountain of tests run on me, to reveal nothing.

How do I even describe the crap that I feel without sounding like it's in my head?

"Are we done, Emerson?"

She exhales a heavy sigh and smiles. "No, but I get the feeling you're done talking to me about it."

"I have work to do."

I spend much of the morning filing, and the paperwork keeps mounting up, with lots of receipts for Blue Sky Resort.

There's a ton of hotel receipts, which make little sense since the resort is only a few minutes from here.

"Ariella, why are we sending people to the Blue Sky Resort?" I ask over my shoulder as I file the receipts away for tax purposes.

She hurries from her desk, her olive eyes wide and her freckles becoming more pronounced as the color of her cheeks reddens.

The look on her face is fueled by concern.

Did I say something wrong?

"You weren't supposed to see that—" she says and glares at me.

"It was mixed into the stack of papers that I have to file. Why are there dozens of rooms being reserved at the resort? Seems like a weird get-together to have you guys hosting an event."

She gives me a look, but the silence that follows tells me I'm completely off base. "Oh," my eyes light up like I get it, but quite honestly, I have no clue what's going on around here.

Mom is out in the field, doing who knows what. She always keeps me in the dark about her job. Most of it a "need to know" basis, and as an intern, there's a lot I apparently don't need to know.

But Ariella has always been a bit more honest and upfront with me about the job.

"It's a private client; they needed some assistance." Ariella ushers me back to my desk, shutting the filing cabinet where I was shoving all the receipts for the hotel.

"Seems weird, but whatever. If it pays the bills—"

"It doesn't," Ariella says, and then shuts her mouth, perhaps slipping up.

I raise an inquisitive eyebrow at her, and she forces a smile. "It's charity work. Now, go get back to your desk, I've got some more files for you to deal with."

"Wonderful."

During lunch, I sit quietly at the park in the shade and pull up Liam's contact information. Not that he ever gave it to me, but I saved his phone number.

I keep writing him a text and then deleting the contents, unsure what to say.

Finally, I hit the button and call him.

Of course, he doesn't pick up the phone. He probably thinks it's a spam caller.

I shoot him a quick text.

Bristol: Answer your phone, loser.

Liam: Who is this?

Bristol: Your worst enemy. The only girl who can take you down a peg or two.

Liam: Bristol?

Bristol: I hate you.

I hit the call button again, and this time, he picks up.

"Back to your snarky self, I see," Liam says instead of an old-fashioned hello.

"You called my dad!"

Silence ensues for a few seconds. "I may have reached out to him. I was worried about you." There's a softness in his tone, a warmth that shouldn't make me relax, and I fight the urge to feel anything other than anger toward Liam Moretti.

I pinch the bridge of my nose and inhale sharply. "I remember distinctly telling you not to call him."

"I guess I'm not a great listener. I'll work on that for you," he says, his tone a little too chipper this afternoon for me.

"Don't bother. Just ... don't ever call him again."

"I promise not to call him," Liam says a little too quickly.

"Or text him!"

"That, I can't promise."

I bite my tongue and reach for my bottle of water, taking a sip. "Why the hell not? Why do you have to be so irritating, Liam?"

"I like it when you say my name, Firebreather." His breath is throaty, sending my heart soaring and my pussy fluttering.

What the hell is he doing to me?

Irritated, I snarl at him. "Oh, fuck off." I end the call, hoping I left him speechless. But it seems to me he left me that way, and I'm not even the tiniest bit happy about it.

He immediately calls me back, but I send it straight to voicemail.

I'm not talking to Liam.

Not now.

Not ever if it were up to me.

I head back to the office, and Jaxson hovers beside Ariella's desk. I try not to stare. It took me a few weeks to realize they were even married; I guess I'm not the brightest crayon when it comes to relationships, at least other people's.

I stalk over to my desk, sit, and begin fumbling through the pages of files that need to be sorted.

Jaxson wanders over to my desk. It's rare that he asks me for anything. Usually, he gets what he needs from Ariella, and if she requires additional help, then I'm her assistant.

"Grab your stuff, I want you to tag along with me today."

"What?" My eyes widen, but I grab my purse and hurry after Jaxson as he leads me out to his SUV. "Is this about Em?" I ask and glance at Jaxson as I climb into the front seat of his vehicle.

"No. Why?" He starts the engine of the vehicle and yanks on his seatbelt.

"No reason," I say, hoping that he's not lying to me. Mom had surprised me this morning, knowing about the emergency room visit, and Jaxson is the absolute best when it comes to digging into people's personal lives. I try to relax, but I'm failing miserably at it. "Where are we going?" I ask.

"You ask a lot of questions." He glances at me as sweat beads my forehead.

Jaxson cranks the air conditioning on full blast inside the car. "Ariella mentioned you were curious about some of our charity work." He lets that word hang in the air for a moment longer than necessary. "You're a little flushed, are you feeling all right?" he asks.

"Fine." I shrug it off. The heat hates me, but it's not anything Jaxson needs to concern himself with; it's my problem.

"Okay, good. What I'm going to show you this afternoon, you have to use discretion."

"I know, just like all the files. Don't ever share anything I see outside of the office."

Jaxson eyes me before returning his attention to the road and pulling away from the office. "No, Bristol, don't ever discuss any of this with anyone—inside or outside of the office."

Same difference.

"Yes, of course." I sit taller and nod, eager that he trusts me. "Where are we heading?"

"Blue Sky Resort."

The ride is mostly in silence, Jaxson turning up the radio, listening to oldies music that he must have enjoyed when he was my age.

A lifetime ago.

He's about my dad's age, maybe a little older. The man is ripped, though, like front cover of a sexy magazine, and if I were into older guys, he'd definitely be hot. There is also a ruggedness to him, and his level of confidence is off the charts.

"How'd you and Ariella meet?" The question slips out before I realize what I've asked, and my eyes widen.

He slowly turns his head, glaring at me. "That's not an appropriate question for your boss."

"Right, sorry. I just ... you both seem like opposites. You're broody and she's sunny."

That cracks a grin on his face. I don't recall ever seeing my boss smile before. He's usually got that rough scowl etched onto his face. The worry lines might as well be tattoos on him.

Although he has quite a few of those on his arms and the one that I can see peek from the collar on his shirt down his neck.

Turns out, I might have a thing for bad boys.

But is Jaxson a bad boy?

He's more of a do-gooder around Breckenridge, but I've heard the stories. He also gets his hands a little dirtier than he should.

Anything to save a damsel in distress. I swear that should be the man's motto or maybe the company's motto.

"Ariella has her own ... unique personality," he says, and I swear there's a hint of a smile. Jaxson shifts in his seat, and as quickly as the tiny grin appears, it vanishes.

"Well, I like her," I admit. "She's a really great boss. Not that you're not great. I appreciate the opportunity that you've given me to intern for you guys this summer." Oh gosh, I'm rambling. I tend to do that when I'm nervous.

Jaxson laughs under his breath, it's deep and throaty. "Noted. You go back to school soon."

"Next week." Technically, the other college kids move back into the dorms this week and school starts the following week. I'm already living there, which makes this commute a bit of a drag to work for Eagle Tactical. Mom and Dad offered to let me stay with them over the summer, it'd be a shorter ride to work, but living with them and having to follow their house rules and curfew all over again, no thanks.

"You are always welcome to come back, winter break, or next summer if you're looking for work."

"Thank you."

We pull up in front of the resort. I've been here a few times growing up, during winter break, when Dad took the private jet for Christmas and flew us to the resort to go skiing. It's like Dad had a love affair with the town.

Or maybe it was because of Emerson.

It's summer now, and the property is rather empty. It seems isn't much to do at the resort off season.

I follow Jaxson inside, and he leads me to the elevator. "Have you met my daughter, Izzie, yet?"

I shake my head and step into the elevator with him. "No, I don't believe so."

He presses the button for the fifth floor, and the elevator ride up is in awkward silence. Once we reach the fifth floor, he steps out first, and I follow while he retrieves a keycard.

Why the hell is he taking me to a hotel room?

My stomach tumbles, and I slow down, letting him walk ahead.

"Jaxson, what are we doing here?"

He's given me no indication that he's ever been interested in me in *that* way. I unclasp my purse and dig my hand in, reaching for my cell phone.

It's not like I have mace or a weapon with me.

Besides, Jaxson Monroe is twice my size and a hell of a lot stronger. The only thing I have going for me is I'm well aware that this whole situation feels off.

"It's for a private client," he says, without so much as glancing at me over his shoulder.

Yeah, sure it is.

I stop walking and glance at my phone.

Mom never mentioned her boss being a creeper. But maybe he has a thing for younger girls and Mom just isn't young enough for him? Maybe she doesn't know. How could she really know her boss if she spent years in a field office in New York and their main office was in Breckenridge?

If I'm wrong ... no, how could I be wrong?

Why would my boss be bringing me to a hotel room at a resort, key card in hand?

I flip through my phone, my hands trembling as I accidentally hit call on the last caller on my phone.

Liam Moretti.

His name lights up on my phone, and my eyes widen.

Shit.

This just went from bad to worse.

"Bristol, let's go." Jaxson's voice booms from down the hall, and his hand is poised with the keycard as he reaches to unlock the door.

"Why are you bringing me to a hotel room?" I ask, my voice catching in my throat. "I'm not interested in you like that, Jaxson. You're married. I'm ... your employee."

"Bristol!" Liam's voice echoes through the phone. He's loud, and my eyes widen and the room sways.

Oh, fuck.

I stumble backward down the hallway, losing my footing. My stomach is in my throat as nausea sets a course, and my vision peppers with stars and darkness as I reach for the wall.

"Not again," I mutter, my legs giving out as I crumble to the ground, blacking out.

Lying on the ground, my eyelids flutter open, staring up at Jaxson, who is hovering over me, concern evident in his eyes. His brow is knitted, and he shoves the keycard into his pocket and retrieves his phone. "Maybe we should call an ambulance for you."

There's a muffled voice from beside me, and I reach for my phone, noticing Liam is still on the call.

Shit.

"I'm fine," I say into the line, and then hang up.

I don't want to talk to Liam.

I really don't like the way Jaxson is staring at me, either.

I push myself to sit, and I feel the tremors pass through me uncontrollably.

Jaxson's arm is on my shoulder. "You shouldn't get up yet. You just passed out."

"Not my first rodeo," I grumble.

"Bend your knees and wiggle them. Try to get the blood flow back up to your heart," Jaxson rattles off orders. He reaches into his pocket for his phone. "Should I call your mom?"

My eyes widen with embarrassment. Of course, I don't want my mom showing up when I'm at work, even though she works for Jaxson too. It's still humiliating!

"For the record," Jaxson stares at me, "I wasn't inviting you up to a hotel room to do anything salacious. Our clients are being housed in several rooms for their safety."

I wipe the beads of sweat from my forehead.

“Yeah, I totally knew that,” I say and force a smile, but I’m still not entirely convinced it wasn’t an overreaction.

It could be an excuse.

I haven’t seen or met the clients he’s referring to yet.

My phone rings, and I ignore it, rejecting the caller. I let the call go straight to voicemail.

Another minute later, it’s ringing again.

I do the same thing.

By the third time it starts ringing, I swear Jaxson is glaring at me.

“Do you want to answer that? It might be important.”

“It’s not,” I mutter and sit myself up, leaning against the wall.

“How about I grab you something to drink?” Jaxson offers.

“Yeah, water would be good.”

"Stay there, okay?" Jaxson watches me intently, and I finally nod. He hurries down the hallway in the direction of the room he was heading toward earlier, retrieves the room key, and then heads inside.

"Clients, my ass," I mutter.

He was totally planning on trying to get me to hook up with him in that room.

Pervert.

A minute later, Jaxson and a younger girl with dark hair and the same inset eyes as Jaxson come hurrying my way.

Is that his daughter he mentioned? The resemblance is uncanny.

What kind of sick game was he planning on in the hotel room ... unless I'm wrong and it wasn't anything nefarious he had planned.

The room spins and my cheeks feel hot, realizing I may have made a big deal out of nothing.

The brunette is maybe a few years older than I am, and she bends down to my level, offering me a bottle of water. "Do you need me to open it?"

"I can do it." Trembling, I reach for the bottle, and she plops down, sitting beside me, her back against the wall.

"I'm Izzie," she says, introducing herself as she hands me the water bottle.

"Bristol."

"How often do you faint?" Izzie asks, and when I struggle to open the bottle because of the tremors, she undoes the lid for me.

I dig into my purse to pull out an electrolyte flavor packet.

"Here, let me," Izzie says and takes the packet, tearing the foil open and dumping the contents into the water before reattaching the lid and shaking the contents.

"I could have shaken it up," I say with a laugh.

"I'm sure. It's not a big deal. I've helped Ella with hers."

"Who's Ella?" I ask.

"Ariella, my mom."

"Now that we're all acquainted," Jaxson says and glances from me to his daughter, "how are things with the girls?"

The girls?

"They're doing as well as can be expected. We've managed to find a few of those who have families searching for them," Izzie says, "but some of the girls don't want to go back home."

"If it's not safe for them, then we need to fully vet their placement into a foster home," Jaxson says.

Izzie nods. "I know the drill. It's just heartbreaking to hear what they've gone through and now some of them only have each other. Separating them seems cruel."

Jaxson bends down to our level. He rests a hand on his daughter's shoulder. "What was cruel is what was done to them. We're just trying to help them the best way that we can now."

My brow pinches. What are they talking about? What girls?

"Maybe bringing Bristol along wasn't the right call," Jaxson says, glancing me over. "I'm going to drive her back to the office, unless you want me to drop you off at home?"

"Great Falls is a trek from here. Besides, you've got work to do. Don't let me keep you. I'll grab the bus."

Jaxson shakes his head. "Not after what just happened here. The air conditioning on the bus is subpar, and if you're anything like my wife, you're going to be struggling for the rest of the day. Let me guess, after the tremors cease, you'll have one hell of a migraine?"

"How'd you know?" I'm lucky if that's the only setback. Saturday, I kept passing out, like my body couldn't ever recover. It was the first time I didn't have a migraine after fainting, but I also had been so preoccupied and fighting with Liam that my blood pressure was probably the highest it's ever been in my life.

"Ariella is the queen of fainting. She's doing better, once we got an actual diagnosis for her condition." Jaxson glances me over. "Let me know when you're feeling capable of standing, and Izzie and I can help you back down to the car."

"Mom has a plethora of abbreviations, stuff that's supposed to be super rare, but it's crazy how many people she's met over the past couple years who share the same or similar conditions," Izzie says.

"Rarely diagnosed," Jaxson corrects his daughter. "It's only rare because doctors aren't knowledgeable on all the latest research and symptoms. I'm sure it's just a coincidence. Fainting can happen for all sorts of reasons, but maybe you should talk to Ariella about it."

The door down the hallway opens and a teenage girl in sweatpants and a t-shirt pokes her head out of the hotel room. "Izzie, can we have pizza for dinner?"

Another girl, who looks a little younger, pops her head out next. "With pepperoni, please."

"Of course," Jaxson answers for Izzie. "We'll order it in a few minutes. Go back in the room, and don't open the door for anyone. Remember?"

The door clicks, and I can't help but wonder what the hell is going on around here.

"I'm ready to stand." It's obvious that I'm just getting in the way. Jaxson and Izzie have work to do, and I don't want to be a hindrance.

The two of them help me to my feet, and they both keep an arm around me as I sway slightly. Jaxson could probably carry me on his own, but I get the distinct feeling he wants his daughter around to prove that he's not trying to take advantage of me.

And I feel even more like shit thinking that he'd been trying to hook up with me. Clearly, I was wrong.

There were the receipts from earlier that I'd asked Ariella about.

They walk me to the elevator, but this time there's more chatter, at least between them. Jaxson hits the down button.

"Oh, Dad, I forgot to tell you. I gave this woman your business card yesterday. Do I get a commission if you book her for private investigative work?" Izzie asks. She wiggles her eyebrows excitedly.

"We'll discuss it later, but I don't see why you can't get a signing bonus for bringing in new clients."

They keep their arms locked around me as we head into the elevator. Jaxson presses the button for the lobby, and they lean me back against the wall, while both still keeping an arm around me to make sure I don't hit the ground.

"Oh good. The girl had a little kid. I overheard them at the police station when I had to stop in, and it was about the Ricci crime family."

Jaxson's hold on me tightens, and I wince and hiss.

He loosens his grip only slightly. "We are not investigating the Ricci family. They're off-limits," Jaxson says. "Absolutely not."

"But it looked like she might have had evidence, and she had a kid with her," Izzie says, her voice slightly whiny. "Come on, Dad. If she calls, we can't just turn her down."

"We can, and we will." Jaxson clears his throat.

"The Ricci family?" I repeat, although I thought the words were in my head, I realize I've spoken them aloud. "As in Luca Ricci, the hockey player for Evergreen University's Narwhals?"

I probably wouldn't even know who he was if my dad hadn't played hockey. I've been following the sport, and since I go to the Predators' games at Great

Falls, I've seen Luca play against our team, and he's good.

"We are not having this discussion here or, quite frankly, anywhere." Jaxson's voice is firm and his tone sharp.

The elevator dings, and we step out together, the two of them escorting me to Jaxson's vehicle. He starts the engine with his key fob as we approach the vehicle. I climb into the front seat, but wait a beat to shut the door. It's stifling inside the car.

Jaxson gives a hug goodbye to Izzie before he climbs into the car.

"I'm driving you home. It's your choice whether it's to your parents' house or back to campus," Jaxson says.

"You're going to drive me all the way back to New York?" I joke.

Jaxson doesn't laugh. "The cabin your parents bought in town."

I raise an eyebrow, the world around me spinning. Thankfully, I'm seated on my ass, or I might be on the ground in a few seconds.

"They bought that place?"

News to me.

Thanks, Mom and Dad for keeping secrets once again.

I thought Mom had been renting the cozy little cabin while working in town. I rub at my forehead, a headache coming on. "Why did you bring my mom back to town?" I know it's not my place to ask, but the question still falls from my lips all the same.

I'd assumed the workload here had been too much, and they needed her help in the short term. But she'd been here nearly a year.

Had I been wrong?

EIGHT

LIAM

I swear, just thinking about *her* makes my phone buzz.

"Hello?" I'm hesitant to answer, but I also want to hear her voice.

Bristol's voice sounds far away, almost muffled, but I still make out the words clear enough.

"Why are you bringing me to a hotel room? I'm not interested in you like that, Jaxson. You're married. I'm ... your employee."

My stomach drops and I shout, making sure that she can hear me. "Bristol!" I need her to give me something else to go on, some way to find her if she needs help.

A hotel.

What hotel?

Where is she?

Who the hell is Jaxson?

There's silence on the other end and I don't like not knowing what's happening.

Her mumbled response comes closer to the phone, "Not again," she mutters, and then there's a loud thud.

Did she fall?

Did her phone hit the ground?

What the hell is going on?

"Bristol!" I try again, but she's not responding.

Silence fills the space, and then a male voice sounds a bit closer to the phone but not directly into the line. "Maybe we should call an ambulance for you."

There's rustling and then a few soft gasps that I'd recognize anywhere.

Bristol.

"I'm fine," she answers and ends the call.

Shit.

Is she fine? Or is she in trouble?

She wouldn't have called me if things were fine. Her boss was taking her to a hotel room. My stomach tangles into a knot just imagining all the grotesque things he might force her to do.

Bristol could be at any hotel in Great Falls, Breckenridge, or another neighboring town.

She wasn't specific enough for me to know where to find her.

I try to call her back, but it goes immediately to voicemail. The same happens after the second and, again, the third time. I don't bother leaving her a message. I do, however, send her a text.

Where are you? Are you okay?

She ignores my text, or maybe she doesn't see it.

Either way, she doesn't answer me. Do I reach out to

her father? That's one sure-fire way to guarantee she hates me.

"I've got to head out." I slip on my shoes and grab my keys by the door.

"Where are you in a rush to?" Nova asks, watching with rapt curiosity.

"I think Bristol is in trouble."

"Good luck!" Nova calls behind me and glances at Ashton. "Who is Bristol?"

I slam the door shut and hurry to my car. I try calling my sister; maybe Sophia can help. She could keep an eye on Bristol's room, make sure that she's not home and playing some cruel trick on me.

"Hey," Sophia answers, her voice warm and sunny. My twin is almost always in a better mood than I am.

"Can you do me a solid and check if Bristol is home?"

"That depends, do you have a crush on her?" Sophia asks.

My mouth opens and snaps shut. I ignore her question. "She called me in a state of panic and then hung up on me. I need to make sure it wasn't her being a brat and prank calling me."

"I don't think Bristol would do that," Sophia says, and I hear the door close behind her. "But I'm walking to the elevator. It'll take me a couple of minutes to get to her dorm. Do you want me to call you back or text you?"

"Call me, I'm driving." I hang up and then try Bristol again.

She doesn't answer. I'm not sure why I expect that she would.

I don't leave a message and I call her father.

Yep, she's going to kill me.

"Hello?" Kyler Greyson's voice holds a hint of curiosity as he answers the call. At least one Greyson is willing to talk with me.

"Sir, this is Liam Moretti. I reached out to you the other day about your daughter."

"Yes, I remember." There's a rustling of papers in the background and then a short pause. "Is everything all right with Bristol?"

"I'm concerned," I admit. "She called me sounding quite panicked about her boss taking her to a hotel room."

"Excuse me?" There's a gruffness exuding from his tone.

"I don't know what's going on, but she won't call me back and I'm concerned."

"As am I," Kyler grunted. "Did she happen to mention who she was with at work?"

"Jaxson," I say, recalling his name.

"Fucking Monroe," Kyler grumbles. "I swear, if he touches my baby girl, I'll—" he ends the call without so much as a goodbye.

NINE

JAXSON

Against better judgement, I agree to take Bristol back to her dorm. I'd prefer to drive her to the cabin where her mother is staying, but she's vehemently against that, and apparently, my mentioning that they bought the place is news to her.

It's been a trying day. I had intended to bring Bristol to the hotel to help with the girls who were brought in from the trafficking ring. My team has been tasked with handling new identities for those who don't have families or safe spaces to go. And those who do have families, we've been quietly reuniting them, one girl at a time.

We have to make sure their families aren't the ones who sold them into the trafficking ring before returning them home.

It's quite a job, and it doesn't exactly pay anything.

Getting mixed up with Dante Ricci isn't my favorite pastime, but the girls need help.

I'm doing it for them.

Also, getting on the wrong side of the local mafia isn't a wise decision. I've lived in Breckenridge long enough to know to steer clear of Dante and his men.

They cause their own brand of havoc, and while I'd rather not get involved in their current mess, at the end of the day, it's for the right cause.

The girls are the priority and going to the police would make things worse for Dante's men.

Why do I care?

Let's just say we all have secrets of our own, and some are best left buried six feet under.

I owe him.

And his cause is justifiable. I wouldn't do it if it weren't.

I do still have morals.

Besides, if I don't help the girls, they could still be in danger. And our local police force is no match for the mafia—Dante's or anyone else's, for that matter.

And I'm convinced whoever trafficked the girls brings far more trouble than Dante would think to bring to town. To me, it wreaks of the cartel, but it could be an opposing mafia family or bratva pushing into the area.

I'm staying out of the dirty details. I don't want to dig up dirt on an investigation that could get my men and my family in further danger.

Protecting the girls, though, it's a noble pursuit, which is why I agreed to it.

"Why did you bring my mom back to town?" Bristol stares at me while I focus on the road.

"Isn't that something you should ask your mother?" I glance at her briefly.

The girl has a bit of hostility and quite clearly a temper under that quiet persona I've seen the past couple of months at the office.

"I'm asking you," Bristol glares.

Fair enough. I don't have any reason to keep secrets regarding Emerson coming back to work in our main office.

"She requested a transfer and to close the New York field office where we operate."

"No," Bristol gasps. "She wouldn't do that."

"She would if she were concerned about you." Had she not realized the entire reason Emerson chose to move out to Breckenridge was to be closer to her daughter? To watch over her?

It couldn't have been easy being apart from her husband, but they make it work. I'd do anything for my children, Izzie and Olivia. They're both grown, twenty-three and twenty, but they're still my children.

"Why would she be concerned..." her voice trails off as my phone rings and my dashboard lights up with the caller's information.

Kyler Greyson.

"My dad is calling you?"

I haven't talked to Bristol's father in quite some time. While Declan had arranged the original contract with him to hire Emerson more than a decade ago, I'd been the one to originally set up his security system in the house prior. We'd met when he was still playing hockey in New York City for the Ice Dragons.

I hit the answer phone button on the steering wheel. "This is Jaxson."

"You and I will have words if something has happened to my daughter."

"I'm with her right now if you'd like to talk to her. I'm driving her back to campus."

"What the hell is going on, Jaxson?" Anger exudes from Kyler's voice, and I shift in my seat.

"Perhaps your daughter would be the best one to explain everything to you."

Bristol opens her mouth and then closes it.

I raise an eyebrow at her before returning my full attention to the road.

"I just had a dizzy spell at the hotel." Bristol exhales loudly and folds her arms across her chest. "I'm fine. You don't need to be calling my boss asking about me, Dad."

I smile at her little scolding to her father.

Cute.

"I'm concerned when I get a phone call that you were at a hotel with your boss!" Kyler is like a train at full-speed, unable to slow. "Jaxson, do you want to tell me what the hell you're doing bringing *my daughter* to a hotel?"

I shift, albeit uncomfortably, and realize how this actually looks. I laugh under my breath. "I see how this could be construed as something nefarious, but I can assure you that I was bringing your daughter to meet with our clients, who are being housed off-site for their protection. I thought she could help with some arrangements, but clearly, it was too much for her."

Bristol is shooting me daggers, but I ignore it. I'm more concerned about one of my best paying clients, Kyler Greyson. Not to mention that his wife works for me, and when she gets wind, I'll get another earful at the office.

"Too much for me?" Bristol chokes and sneers at me. "That's not fair. You bring me to a hotel room, what was I supposed to think?"

My jaw drops.

She was overreacting.

Maybe I was under-reacting in bringing her with me. I could have brought Emerson along, perhaps I should have, but that's all in the past.

"I won't make that mistake again," I grit between clenched teeth.

You do a favor for someone, hire their college kid for a summer, and this is the thanks I get?

I take a few deep breaths and release my tightened grasp on the steering wheel as I take the exit toward Great Falls. We're still thirty minutes out, and this drive is growing all the more tense.

"Anything else, Kyler?" I'm hesitant to even ask, but I also want this conversation over.

Kyler clears his throat then answers. "Yes, what was that earlier about my daughter having a dizzy spell?"

"She fainted in the hotel hallway." I glance at Bristol and her eyes widen in horror, like I just revealed that she's pregnant to her father.

My brow pinches and I glance her over.

She isn't pregnant, is she?

"It's nothing, Dad, just another dizzy spell," Bristol quips, making it known to her father that she's fine.

"Fainting isn't a dizzy spell, Bristol. And this is the second day in a row."

"It was Saturday night when I went to the Emergency Room," Bristol counters. "Well, Sunday morning by the time I left, but it's not a big deal."

"It is a big deal." Kyler's voice is gruff. "Mom and I are concerned about your health. Are you having issues in class?"

"I don't know, Dad. It's summer break!"

I roll my lips and keep my mouth shut. There's no sense in me getting between those two. I'd offer her my phone to take the call with a little more privacy, but it's in my pocket, and quite frankly, I'm slightly amused at the antics between those two.

She's flustered and frustrated.

I can only imagine Kyler up in arms, not being able to do anything.

Perhaps that's why Emerson decided to move out here? Had she sensed something was off with their daughter?

Kyler grumbles and I suppress a smirk. Oh yeah, he's definitely pissed.

"You've been fainting a lot, Bristol. That's not normal. I'm going to bring in a specialist, someone to make sure everything is all right."

"Dad!"

I glance at Bristol. I should keep my mouth shut, but I can't. "Listen, my wife has some health anomalies as well. We found a good autonomic neurologist for Ariella. The doctor is hard to get an appointment with, but Ariella can reach out and try to get an appointment for Bristol. She's the best in the area, and I'm sure if Ariella reaches out, then she can get Bristol in for a work-up. She's in Billings, which is a six-hour drive—"

"That's not a problem. I can have my jet fly her anywhere she needs for the best care," Kyler says.

Bristol is glaring at me. "I don't need a *work-up*. I'm fine. I just faint when it gets a bit warm. I probably need to drink more electrolytes."

"What are some of your other symptoms?" I ask.

"I really don't want to do this," Bristol huffs.

Kyler, however, ignores his daughter's request. "She's always been dehydrated easily. She gets migraines, faints, has had some balance issues, low blood pressure. When Bristol stands up too fast, she blacks out for a few seconds."

When I first met Ariella, there hadn't been a diagnosis for her condition. It had just been weird symptoms that plagued her at the most inopportune time, like when we were dancing at the bar together.

What I thought had been one drink too many had been entirely something else.

Bristol quips, "You forgot the nausea, irritability, and the fact that my heart feels like it's pounding out of my chest. Plus, the stomach problems, do you want to hear about my diarrhea, too, and how I can eat one food one day, and the next, I can barely make it to the bathroom in time?"

The similarities to her and Ariella are uncanny.

"I told you I thought going away to college wasn't a good plan," Kyler says, concern in his tone.

"That's what you'd like, me to go to school in New York and live at home. No, thank you! I'm quite happy at Great Falls." Bristol is a bit of a spitfire.

I bite my tongue. I don't think my interjecting is going to help the two of them right now.

"Is that why Mom is working in Breckenridge?" Bristol asks. "Is it because of me?"

There's a soft sigh on the other end of the phone. "Mom is there in case you need someone, and of course, to work. We just want to be close to you."

"I'm nineteen, Dad! You have to learn to let go eventually."

He grumbles and clears his throat. "Jaxson, send me the information for that physician you recommended."

"I'll have Ariella call their office and also give Emerson all the details. Does that work for you?"

"Yeah, appreciated."

We end the call, and Bristol is glaring at me. She's probably relieved it's the last week she's scheduled to work for me and school is resuming, because I have a feeling it'd be tense as hell in the office with her around.

Kind of like when Ariella first began working for me.

Except Ariella and I had a constant hard-on for each other, and well, that is definitely not the case with Bristol.

She's practically my youngest daughter's age.

I'm relieved when I arrive at her campus, and she directs me toward the dorms. I pull up out front. "Do you need help getting inside?" I offer.

"I've got it, Jaxson. Thanks for the ride." She hurries out of the car into the blazing heat, and I just hope that she'll be all right on her own.

"Stay hydrated!" I shout at her as she slams the door shut and gives me a forced *fuck you* smile.

TEN

LIAM

Driving up toward Great Falls, I do the unthinkable and try calling Bristol, again.

"You really need to stop calling," Bristol bellows at me, and I breathe a sigh of relief.

She's not dead. That's a good sign.

"Where are you?" I ask.

"My boss just dropped me off; I'm heading into the dorms right now."

My hands knuckle the steering wheel. "Right. Are you okay? Did you faint again?" Worry creeps up inside me, and I can't help but wonder what the hell is going on with her.

"I'm fine."

Somehow, I doubt that.

She huffs and her next question makes my heart race. "Did you call my dad again?" There's an accusation in her tone, but the thing is, she's absolutely on point.

Because I did call her dad.

But I don't want to admit it.

Silence fills the space, which gives her the answer she's looking for it seems.

"You're a jerk," Bristol says, and I wince. "I can fight my own battles, Liam."

"Can you? Remember, you called *me* from the hotel."

I imagine her stomping around, throwing a tantrum at the realization that she reached out to me first. I'm just checking up on her.

"It was a mistake. I was trying to call someone else—anyone else," she hisses.

"Well, you probably should remove me from your contact list, so your finger doesn't accidentally slip and call me again."

"You're such an asshole!" she seethes.

A wicked smile spreads across my face.

"Yes, one you keep on speed dial. What does that say about you, Firebreather?"

She groans excessively and then huffs into the phone, making it clear she's irritated with me. I'm glad I can still rile her up.

"I hate you, Liam Moretti!"

I shrug off her words. "I know, you've already called me an asshole. Do you want some more hurtful names you can shout at me over the phone? For the record, I'm glad to know you're safe and everything is fine." I end the call, refusing to let Bristol get the last word.

All I was doing was trying to help.

It's not my fault she called, freaked out, and then hung up.

She wouldn't answer and tell me what's really going on.

Not that she explained anything to me now, other than that she hates my guts.

That's not anything new or exciting in the life of Bristol Greyson. She's always hated me.

I call Sophia, wanting to give her an update.

"No need to check on Bristol," I inform my sister. I make a right and then turn around, heading back toward the house. There's no reason for me to drive all the way up Great Falls. I'm clearly not wanted there.

"Did you hear from her?" Sophia asks. Her voice is relaxed and calm, but it doesn't settle my racing heart or thoughts.

"Yeah, she finally answered my call. Her boss just brought her back to campus." I bite my tongue, not liking that her boss is driving her back to school. Wasn't he the reason she called me? Because he's married and was bringing her to a hotel room? The whole situation screams ick.

"Her boss is driving her home?" Sophia asks. It's clear that she's as confused as I am.

"Yeah, I don't know, the whole situation has been shit. She calls me sounding panicked, and next thing I know, she hangs up and doesn't return my calls. I could barely get an answer from her on any of it. I'm done," I growl, frustration irking me. With Bristol, it's always irritation and annoyance. She's not making my life any easier.

Why do I care what happens to her?

She's made it clear she despises me.

"I'm sure it's nothing," my sister reassures me. "I'll stop by and check on her this afternoon, see what I can find out."

"Don't bother. She's not worth the headache," I mutter.

I head back into the house, Nova staring at me with a perplexed frown. "You're home already. Everything okay?"

"No. Yes. I don't know," I grumble and flop down on the sofa next to her.

Ashton is sitting on the floor, stretching while Zeke climbs onto his back like a jungle gym and he flips him forward, catching him.

"Sounds complicated. So, tell me about this girl, Bristol."

ELEVEN

NOVA

Classes resume, and already, I'm in over my head with the course load. Ashton and I are both taking Criminology together. We're in the same class, which might explain why I'm failing.

I suppose I've been paying more attention to him than the lessons.

He's easy on the eyes, and I keep daydreaming about what I'd do to him with a pair of handcuffs.

Well, that's not the only fantasy of Ashton fleeting through my mind, but it's the most prominent in this class. It doesn't hurt that he bought a pair of furry pink handcuffs this week, but we haven't gotten time to use them.

It's like I have an itch that desperately needs scratching.

Distracted?

Understatement of the century, and to top it off, the teacher also loves to give us pop quizzes, so it's not like I can study before the exam. Ashton glances at the giant red *F* on my paper as the teaching assistant returns our quizzes.

"Shit," I curse under my breath.

Ashton's brow is furrowed, and he nudges my arm. "Don't worry, we'll study tonight."

"You have practice," I remind him. I liked early summer, spending time with Ashton, without worrying about school or his training camp for hockey.

Now, it's like I have to compete for his attention, but at least it's not against other girls.

The teaching assistant, Henry, grabs the seat next to me, as we're in the back row against the wall.

I continue to take notes, trying my best to pay attention after the lousy grade.

I start packing up my things as class ends, and Henry leans toward me, invading my personal space. His voice is low, rumbly, and barely above a whisper, like what he's saying is meant only for my ears. "Do you want to grab lunch together? I could help you study this evening or another night at my place."

My mouth drops, and I'm stunned.

Henry has spoken a handful of words to me, but it's always a polite hello or if he can borrow a pencil. He's never blatantly asked me to grab a meal with him—and he's the teaching assistant for this class. Isn't that against some kind of code of conduct?

Ashton is staring at me, wondering what the hell is going on, and I don't blame him.

I force a reassuring smile his way, and then my face falls slack as I stare at Henry. "I have plans with my boyfriend, Ashton, for lunch." I shove the rest of the papers haphazardly into my backpack and zip it up, wanting to get the hell out of there, pronto.

I'm a bit disheveled after what Henry asked me. It's not like he suggested a study group he was hosting.

He asked me about studying with him, at night, at his place.

I'm definitely *not* reading too much into it.

"And what about that study session, just you and me?" Henry asks, his throat raspy as he leans closer. "I can make sure your grade gets turned around."

I'll bet he can.

"Excuse me?" Ashton overhears Henry. My boyfriend grabs my arm, pulling me behind him as he steps forward, face-to-face with Henry.

Oh, shit.

"She already told you she's not interested," Ashton growls at Henry. "Quit asking my girlfriend if she needs a tutor. If someone's going to help her, it's going to be *me*."

I rest a hand on Ashton's arm, gently trying to tug him back. I don't want him getting into a fight with the teaching assistant.

Ashton slings his bag over his shoulder and intertwines his hand with mine. "You ready to grab lunch, babe?"

Is Ashton trying to rub Henry's nose in the fact that I'm not single, and he's claiming me? Ordinarily, I'd find it hot and a turn on, but I'm a little worried that Henry might take it out on me next time he's forced to grade one of my assignments.

We head out of the classroom and Ashton is right beside me, nudging me as we walk to lunch. "Can you believe that asshole? We should go over his head, to the professor or maybe the dean in his department. Someone should be aware that he's hitting on the students!"

I tug Ashton's hand, making him pause as I stop.

"I don't want you making things worse for me."

"Did you hear him?" Ashton stares at me, mouth agape. "He was hitting on you, and I'm worried if you don't do as he demands, it'll affect your grade. He's slime, Nova!"

I try to shake off the anxiety prickling under my skin. "It's just one quiz. It's not worth that much of our grade. Don't worry." Although it isn't the first pop quiz I failed in class.

"It's the next exam I'm worried about for you," Ashton says. He tugs me into the dining hall, and we both grab food at opposite ends. He stands in line for a sandwich while I grab a burger and fries.

I glance around while waiting in line, making sure Henry isn't anywhere to be seen.

My stomach is doing somersaults.

I've never run into him outside of class in the past, but it doesn't mean he may not have followed me. He's on campus, he eats in the same dining hall, at least at some point, I imagine he does. Hopefully, not today, during this lunch hour.

After I grab my burger and fries, I snatch up a table for Ashton and me to sit. He's still getting his sandwich, the line a little longer since they're making his by hand.

I grab my backpack and pull out my criminology textbook. Every extra minute that I cram has to be beneficial. And there's zero chance that I'd study with Henry alone. I'm not even sure it's worth continuing the class that I'm in.

My food sits untouched as my eyes glaze over the text from today's lesson.

Ashton strolls up to the table and shuts the textbook on me.

“What was that for?” I growl.

“Study tonight, when I’m at practice.” At our table, he grabs the seat across from me. “Eat your lunch.”

Sighing, I take the burger and take a bite.

“Happy?” I mumble.

He unwraps his sandwich. “I’d be happier if that douche didn’t ask you out in Criminology. What the hell was that?”

I’m pretty sure his question is rhetorical.

I merely shrug and shove my textbook back into my bag. “I don’t know. Asking me out is weird, right?”

Ashton glares up at me with a fire behind his dark eyes. “It would be weird not to be attracted to you. But asking you to lunch and to study at his place, highly inappropriate.”

So, Ashton did hear the entire exchange. I hadn’t been sure with how quiet Henry had attempted to be, whispering in my ear.

I grimace, just thinking about it playing over in my head is bothersome.

"I suck at Criminology and now, with the teaching assistant having it out for me, maybe I should drop the class."

"You'll get a W for withdrawn, but it won't affect your GPA. You're past the deadline where it doesn't show up on your transcript, though." Ashton stares seriously at me. "It's up to you. Why'd you pick Criminology to take this semester? Aren't you majoring in Sociology?"

I don't admit that I chose the class because I knew Ashton would be in it. I thought it'd be fun to have class together. It sucks, though, because he's doing a million times better than I am in the class.

His leg nudges me under the table.

"I thought it'd be easy."

Ashton shakes his head and takes another bite of his sandwich. "You took it because I signed up for it. Didn't you?"

"No!" I scoff at his suggestion. "I wouldn't do that." I

glance away then down at my burger, grabbing it and taking a huge bite so I don't have to answer him.

He laughs under his breath. "Good, because that would be reckless, Nova. You need to be taking classes for your major, or at the very least, the gen eds required."

"Criminology was one of the electives that are part of the Sociology curriculum. Chill out. I'm not taking a class just because you're in it. Don't get such a big head, Ashton."

"Right, my mistake." He holds up his hand in mock surrender. "Do you want to try out those handcuffs tonight?" He wiggles his eyebrows at me.

My cheeks burn.

Boy, do I ever.

"Only if I get to lock you up," I quip.

Ashton purses his lips, contemplating my request. "I'll have to think about it. Whether you're a good girl for me for the rest of the day or not."

I snort.

"I'm always a *good girl*," I say with a snicker.

"I don't know about that; more times, you're spice than anything nice."

I grab a fry and pop it into my mouth, staring at him curiously. "I thought you liked a little spice in your life."

"I like you in my life," Ashton admits. There's no hesitation on his part.

His leg slides up mine beneath the table, and my eyes widen.

Anyone could see us, and I'm not giving some spectator a free show!

"Oh my gosh. Quit it!" I scowl at him playfully.

"I'm worried about you. Are you still concerned about Henry?" He takes a bite of his sandwich and waits for me to answer.

I am a bit jolted over the ordeal. My silence only makes him nudge me under the table again, but this time his leg is playing with mine and my eyes widen. "Ashton!"

He grins and stares at me, his gaze never wavering. "I just don't like seeing you upset."

I let out a hefty sigh and grab a bite of my burger. I'm not very hungry, but I try to force it down because I should eat something. After I swallow it down, I grab a sip of water and glance up at him.

"I miss spending time with you. You're at hockey practice all the time and the season is just starting."

The Narwhals play their first game next week, away. It's not that far, Great Falls, but I still hate that he won't be home playing hockey.

Maybe I can convince Harper to come with me, and we'll take the bus, make it a little surprise?

But she has Zeke, which tends to be a fun killer. Not that I don't love that kid, but he has a routine, and if you don't abide by it, he's a little monster.

Ashton gives me a lopsided grin. "You knew when we first started dating that I play hockey. My schedule isn't anything new."

"I just hate it," I confess. "You spend more time with the boys than me. Sorry, I guess I'm just jealous and feeling needy." I avoid his stare and put my burger down on the plate, grabbing a fry instead.

"You're cute, even when you're moody." Ashton is all smiles. "I promise, I can take care of the Henry situation, make him disappear."

I think he's trying to make me laugh.

The worry descends on my face.

He had better be joking.

While I know that Ashton works alongside my father, I'm not particularly thrilled about it.

"You're not going to do anything to Henry," I growl. "He's my problem."

"Anyone who's your problem *is* my problem." Ashton tilts his head, his eyes glancing me over, filled with concern. "And there are other ways to make the problem disappear. Like I said, I can go over his head."

Exhaling heavily, I nod, considering the different options.

I don't want to get him fired. At least, not yet. "Let me think on it?"

"As long as that thinking doesn't involve you

studying with another guy," Ashton says and smiles. "Luca and Liam are the only exceptions."

"Luca isn't taking Criminology." He's steering far from those classes.

Ashton shrugs. "Then I guess you'll have to study with me when I get home."

"We can study before dinner," I suggest.

We both have a break in classes and hockey practice is in the evening.

"I miss our weekends and we barely have any nights together. It just ... it sucks."

Ashton reaches across the table for my hand. He intertwines our fingers together. "I'll make time for you. I promise." Ashton means well, but he has a lot going on.

"Thanks." A wayward smile crosses my face, and I push my plate aside, deciding I've eaten enough. My appetite is scarce this afternoon.

"How are things at my parents'?" I ask. He spends more time around them than I do lately.

"Dante is still pissed about what went down with Harper. He's been in a foul mood ever since."

I bite down on my bottom lip.

Ashton reaches out, his thumb stroking my mouth, tugging my lip free with his thumb. "It's your parents' house, you can join me if you want—"

"I'd prefer to avoid Dante if he's been in a hellacious mood." As much as I want to spend weekends, at least the night, curled up with Ashton, I've been trying to be supportive of Luca and Harper.

Dante has made it clear that she is no longer welcome in their home.

Luca and Harper are also my family.

"Trust me, his mood hasn't gotten any better. Neither has your father's," Ashton admits. "I think he hates me."

"Why? Because we're together?" I hadn't realized Dad knew about us, but now that it's out in the open, I kind of want to flaunt it in their faces.

I've got a bit of trouble written under my skin.

Ashton finishes his lunch and scoots his chair back. I grab my bag and follow him, tossing our trash out on the way out of the dining hall. "Your dad has it out for me."

"What do you mean?" I ask, walking alongside Ashton as he escorts me to my next class.

"I'm dating his daughter. If I fuck up anything in your life, he'll kill me."

I grab his hand and stop walking. We still have plenty of time until the next class. "Has he threatened you?"

"He doesn't like me, Nova. That's threat enough."

"Maybe he just hasn't gotten the opportunity to know you like I do," I say, trying to reason with Ashton.

"I'm fucking his daughter." Ashton stares at me seriously. "He's an overbearing, protective father who worries about his daughter. I don't blame him, but I'm certainly not having family dinners at your parents' house."

What he isn't saying aloud is that my father is *mafia*. That's the reason he's most afraid.

"Never?" I ask, surprised. "You'll never have dinner at my parents' house?"

I wish I'd known Dad was aware of my relationship with Ashton. I would have invited Ashton to stay for dinner and get to know my parents better.

Why had he kept it from me? Not only Ashton, but my father as well?

"When was the last time you had dinner with your parents?" he asks.

It's been months.

He tugs my hand to keep walking so we're not late.

"That's beside the point. I'm not having dinner there because Harper and Zeke aren't invited. I'm boycotting their family dinners. Luca is also my family, and if they can't accept Harper and Zeke, then I'm not showing up."

As I approach the old stone building, Ashton grabs my other hand, pulling me against him. His breath teases my lips apart.

I lean in, wanting to kiss him when he asks, "Do you think Harper would betray the family again?"

My brow pinches, curious why he's asking *me* that question.

I pull back slightly, stunned. "I don't know. I'm surprised she went to the police in the first place. You'd have to ask Luca that question. Why?"

"Come on, you're one of her best friends. She doesn't talk to you about this stuff?" Ashton's question makes my heart turn to ice.

He's not asking out of concern for her.

A breezy gust of autumn air whips past me and I shiver. Dropping Ashton's hands, I take a step back. "Dante asked you to spy on Harper, didn't he?"

TWELVE

ASHTON

It shouldn't come as a surprise to Nova that I'm tasked with keeping a close eye on Harper. It's been that way since she stumbled into the basement nearly a year ago.

I haven't exactly announced that I'm keeping tabs on her for Dante.

Why would I do that?

It's easier to gain her trust and report back to him anything problematic, which hadn't been much until the recent incident with her running off to the police station.

She hasn't spoken about it to me, and Luca seems to have forgiven her.

Something I'm not sure I'd have done.

"Spy on Harper? I mean, if you want to put it so bluntly, then, yes."

Nova folds her arms across her chest and points to the building where her next class is. "I have to go, but this conversation, it isn't done."

My gaze tightens. There's no sense in arguing with Nova and upsetting her.

"Yeah, I'll catch you later." I lean in to give her a kiss, and she turns her head to the side, letting me kiss her cheek.

Oh, fuck, she's pissed.

"Catch you later." I force a smile and watch as she saunters into the building without so much as glancing back at me.

The girl is definitely angry with me.

I head for the crosswalk and wait at the intersection for the light to change. "How was lunch with your little friend?" Henry asks. There's a menacing tone in his voice.

My shoulders tense and I spin around, grumbling under my breath when Henry is staring slightly up at me.

I've got several inches on him.

I wanted to be wrong. I was hoping that perhaps the question was directed at someone else. But it's just the two of us waiting to cross the street.

"Excuse me?" I growl. "My little friend?" What the fuck is he trying to say about Nova?

Henry smirks and tilts his head, staring up at me. "You should let her know, if she wants a passing grade, it's going to take a date with me."

"The hell it will!" I yank his shirt and tug him toward me.

He's lucky I'm not shoving him into the street to get hit by a car.

"What are you—" Henry looks startled as I get up in his face.

"Nova made it crystal clear she isn't interested in you. Leave her the fuck alone!" I shout, spit flying as

I can no longer keep my temper from going off the rails.

“Get your grimy paws off me.” Henry shoves me away and scoffs as he wipes the imaginary dust from his shirt. “I’ll have sex with whomever I damn well please.” The cocky grin on his face is deplorable.

“Nova made it clear to leave her the fuck alone.”

Henry doesn’t stop smiling. “Do you think that’s going to stop me? Girls always like playing hard to get. Nova isn’t any different. Her no absolutely means yes.”

I slam my fist across his face with an uppercut and then knee him in the groin. He doubles over in agony.

Good.

“Touch her and die,” I growl at Henry before I storm across the street, the crosswalk momentarily clear.

“You’ll pay for this!” Henry shouts.

"What happened to your knuckles?" Nova's fingers are featherlight as she grazes the slight discoloration.

I was hoping she wouldn't notice, let alone ask about it, but it's kept the tension between us at bay. I suppose she's forgotten or maybe forgiven me about earlier.

"It's best if you don't ask." I stand and head into the kitchen, grabbing us both a glass of water and a snack. I'm using it as a distraction. We haven't even gotten started, and I'm already bailing on her.

She's going to need help studying if Henry has any say regarding her grades.

I grab a bowl of grapes and two bottles of water, bringing it back to the table to study.

Nova has her books out, taking up most of the table, and I join her, glancing over her latest quiz.

The glaring red *F* irks me, but it's the answers to the quiz I find even more unsettling.

"You've got to be fucking kidding me!"

"What is it?" Nova asks. "I know I screwed up. Don't laugh. I'm asking for your help tutoring me, not making fun of me for being stupid."

My jaw drops. "Nova, you're not stupid." I reach into my bag and retrieve my pop quiz, showing her the answers. "You got each one right. Look."

"What?" Her brow furrows as she stares at me, then reads the answers to my exam. "How can that be?"

"You're better in class than you thought." I exhale loudly and lean back in my chair. "Henry has it out for you. He's a fucking pig." I stand, pacing the length of the room.

"Why would he fail me?" Nova asks. "I don't understand."

"Henry thinks that by failing you, he can somehow get you to fuck him. He's using his position of power. It's disgusting." I run a hand through my hair and tilt my head up at the ceiling.

Think, dammit.

There has to be something we can do to get even with him.

Really stick it to him.

"We should go to the professor or the dean," Nova says.

I glance away from Nova. "Yeah, that's an option..." My voice trails off as I try to come up with another solution.

"Why? Do you have a better suggestion, Ashton?"

"Let me think."

Nova stands from the chair and faces me. "Why is going to the professor a bad idea? They would have to investigate and would keep me from failing the class. And if the professor won't listen, then we take it up with the dean."

I answer her with silence.

"Ashton?" Nova's tone is louder, more forceful. "What aren't you telling me?"

She reaches for my hand, glancing at my bruised hand. "You got this today, recently."

I hate how observant Nova is, that she realizes I wasn't bruised this morning in class or when we were at lunch.

"It doesn't matter." I try to deflect. "Did you happen to keep the other quizzes that you failed?" I ask.

The only papers that Henry is responsible for, as far as I've seen, are the pop quizzes. But that doesn't mean he isn't grading our exams or upcoming midterms.

Nova shakes her head. "I wasn't too happy about the grade. The last two that I failed, I tore up the quizzes as soon as I left the classroom and tossed them in the garbage."

I wrap my arms around her waist, pulling her against me.

"I'm sorry I didn't offer to tutor you sooner." Shame burns me. I should have noticed that Henry had been interested in Nova.

I'd been too swept up in the fact that she's mine to even notice anyone else taking an interest in her—not that Henry had been obvious until today.

What changed?

"Maybe I should drop the class, Ashton. Henry has it out for me, and I can't prove I didn't fail the other quizzes that he graded..."

"No." I'm adamant that dropping the class isn't the answer. "Come on, you and me. The daughter of a mafia enforcer and me, who works for the mafia, can figure this out."

She laughs darkly. "What are you suggesting, Ashton? String him up, torture, interrogate, and then kill him?" There's a smile on her face.

"I'd do all of that for you if it'd make you happy."

She smacks my chest. "You're so full of shit. I love you, but if you hang him, I'll never forgive you for committing murder."

I grab her wrist, intertwining our fingers together. "Did you just say the l word to me?"

Nova's eyes widen, and she turns her back, hurrying to the table to shovel her books and papers into her backpack.

"Nova?" I'm watching with rapt fascination. "I love you too."

The moment is interrupted when the front door slams shut and the house shakes. Frowning, I poke my head around to see Harper holding Zeke in her arms and locking the front door.

"Where the hell is Luca?" Harper shouts.

"He's not home yet," I say. "Do you need something?" I try to defuse the ticking timebomb that is Harper McKenna Ricci.

What the hell happened?

Her hair is a bit disheveled and the fury in her dark brown eyes makes my stomach revolt. I can't even force a smile. There's pain and concern etched all over her face.

"Where's Luca?" she asks again, just as forceful.

Nova comes around the corner, backpack in hand. "He's probably still at class, Harper. What's wrong?" She puts her bag on the floor and walks over to offer to take Zeke, who has a bit rosy cheeks.

"Someone tried to pick up my son today from school."

"Who?" Nova asks the same question that I'm wondering.

"That's what I'd like to know. He wouldn't give his name. Claimed to be Zeke's father." She grinds her teeth and hands Zeke over to Nova.

"Is it possible his biological father showed up?" I ask. Harper has never mentioned the father to me, but

I've done a little digging. Assuming it's the guy she dated in high school, he's not that hard to track down.

"That was my first thought but, no, it's not him. She rolls her lips together and steps closer, staring up at me. "Tell me everything that you and Dante have been working on, Ashton," she demands.

"You know I can't do that."

"You can, and you will. If my son is in danger, I need to know what the hell is going on. No more secrets!"

THIRTEEN

HARPER

Nova comforts Zeke, taking him out of the room while I wait for Ashton to explain what the hell is going on.

He and Luca have been working for Dante for months, keeping secrets, as they always do.

I've let it slide, since the danger seemed to have passed after the last time I was at the Ricci home.

But finding out that a man with a snake tattoo on his neck showed up and tried picking my son up from daycare...

When he wouldn't give his name or show any identification, they called campus security.

The guy fled long before the campus police showed up.

There wasn't much more of a description, other than he was approximately our age, had dark hair, dark eyes, and the tattoo.

My ex would never have let anyone near him with a needle, with his trypanophobia. Besides, he doesn't have dark hair or dark eyes.

Which has me questioning who else would show up for Zeke.

"The man had a snake tattoo." I gesture to my neck. "Do any of Dante's men have that type of tattoo?" Ashton would know; he's worked long enough for Dante.

"No." Ashton folds his arms across his chest. "Any other distinguishing features?"

"Dark hair, dark eyes. They didn't give me a lot to go on, and the security camera feed didn't capture anything. He wore a hat to cover his face from view."

"Of course, he did," Ashton grumbles and glances over his shoulder at Nova, who is standing in the hallway with Zeke, eavesdropping.

"If it's not one of Dante's men, then whoever was after us months ago, they're still out there."

Ashton paces the length of the living room, quiet.

"Ashton?" I need answers.

"I'm thinking!" He huffs, and the front door turns with the lock as it is unclasped.

My heart pounds wildly in my chest when Luca steps inside. "Someone tried to kidnap our son!"

"What?" Luca growls and drops his bag at the front door. "Where is he?"

"He's okay." Nova cuddles Zeke, nuzzling his nose, and he wiggles to get down.

Zeke runs to Luca, and he swiftly lifts him off the ground, pulling him into his arms. Luca thoroughly examines Zeke, inspecting to make sure there's not so much as a fresh scratch or mark on him.

"Whoever it is, he didn't get past the front entrance

at the daycare." I tilt my head, staring at Luca. "Do you know anyone with a snake tattoo on their neck?"

His brow pinches, and immediately, he shakes his head, no hesitation. "No. Is that the description of the guy?"

I recant the physical details I was given to Luca, which isn't much.

Luca and Ashton exchange a quick glance.

"What aren't you telling me?" I shout, demanding to be let in on their little secret. Whatever it is, I don't like being kept in the dark when it involves my family.

"The threat from this past year is dead, but it's possible someone else in the DeLuca family took Massimo's place," Luca says.

"DeLuca family?" I have no idea who they are. "What do they want with *my* son?"

"Probably to get to Dante through you," Ashton guesses. "I suppose they don't realize you two don't get along."

Luca's nose crinkles as he glances at Ashton. "We have an away game this week."

There's a heavy sigh that escapes Ashton's lips. He glances in the direction of the hallway where Nova is standing. She leans against the wall, no longer hiding from the conversation.

"Do you think something might happen when you're gone?" Nova is the first to ask.

"Nothing is going to happen to my family," Luca growls and stalks closer to me, Zeke still in his arms.

I feel his presence before he takes the last stride, coming to stand in front of me. "You're going to stay with Dante while we're away."

Zeke climbs from Luca back into my arms, and I finally put him down, letting him run around the house, convinced that it's safe here.

"What?" My eyes widen. "You're absolutely insane, Luca. Your father hates me, made it clear that I'm not welcome. Are you certain he's not the one behind the abduction? This could all be a revenge plot, a way to teach me a lesson for going to the cops."

He purses his lips, not denying my question. "No one he works with has a snake tattoo. Liam, Ashton, and I are going to be home late after the game. I don't like knowing that it's just the two of you girls alone with Zeke."

Nova steps forward. "I know how to use a gun."

Ashton strides across the room, pulling Nova close against him. "Come to the game with us."

"What about Harper and Zeke?" Nova asks. She smacks Ashton's chest. "I can't believe you'd suggest I leave my best friend and her son behind to go watch your game."

Ashton grabs Nova's wrist after the second smack.

"All three of you," Ashton growls. "Drive Luca's car up to Great Falls and come see the game. Nothing will happen if you're in public. These guys don't operate around out in the open."

"Right. Like they don't strike at grocery stores?" Harper quips, raising an eyebrow.

"That was the parking lot," Ashton says. "The hockey game will have a lot of people and it's an away game. You guys will be safer in Great Falls at the game than here, alone."

"I'll drive us home after the game," Luca agrees, "but

that doesn't solve the issue the next time we're at an away game, none of us will be here to protect you."

"I'll be here." Nova stomps her foot, annoyed that the boys don't seem to pay her any attention.

"Yes, we heard you." Luca glances at Nova. "But you're not exactly the muscle around here."

She glares at Luca and swings her fist at him, trying to prove her point, but he blocks it and shoves her backward up against the wall. Luca glares at Ashton all the while, holding Nova against the wall. "Control your girlfriend!"

"Control your sister!" Ashton shoots back at him.

Nova struggles against his grip, his point clearly made.

He drops his hold on her. "I'll talk to Dante."

Luca can't be serious. I scoff at his suggestion. "You're going to talk to your father, the man who absolutely hates me?" I don't see how Dante is going to help with the situation. If he's not already behind the attempted abduction, he'll make it worse.

"He doesn't hate you," Luca says, but not even he sounds convinced of his own words.

Ashton clears his throat. "I hate to dampen the mood, but we need to grab a quick bite and then head to practice. Coach is going to pissed if we're late."

Luca looks a bit perplexed, and then shakes the cobwebs free. Whatever he's thinking, it's clearly troubling him. I just hope he won't be distracted at practice or tomorrow at their game in Great Falls.

"I'm not leaving Harper and Zeke alone. I'll skip practice," Luca says.

"You can't skip it, coach is still pissed about you missing the last game of last season," Ashton says. He heads toward the door, getting his shoes and coat on.

"Fine, then Harper and Zeke are coming with us. I'm not leaving them alone."

Luca doesn't even ask my input but I'm glad he's taking charge. It makes me feel safe after what happened today. "Okay." I hurry to help Zeke get his shoes on then I do the same while Luca gets ready to head back out the front door.

"We can't go to every practice with you," I remind him. "We're going to have to figure something out."

"This weekend, we'll work on self-defense training," Luca says. "I'm going to teach you the basics to protect yourself and Zeke."

"What about if the assailant has a weapon, like a gun?" He can't honestly expect me to disarm him with some basic self-defense.

"We'll take you to the shooting range," Ashton says. He jabs his thumb in the direction of Luca. "I taught this guy to use a gun. You can't do any worse than Luca on your first day."

I watch from the stands; Nova, Kensley, and I are seated next to each other at the Predators' arena in Great Falls. Zeke has his headphones on to help block some of the noise as he sits on my lap and then squirms, wanting to run around.

We managed to quite easily convince Kensley to join us on the drive. I've seen less and less of her lately, and I miss hanging out together.

She's constantly with Brooks or partying, which I have little interest in doing. Even if I wanted to party, I've got Zeke, which makes it a non-priority.

"Look at your daddy," I say, pointing at the ice as Luca skates on by. We're several rows back, with Predators' fans all around us.

Our little group wears our Narwhals jerseys. We definitely stand out, but there's a speckling of white and teal throughout the arena in a sea of green and black.

"Since when did you and Brooks hook up?" Nova asks, glancing briefly at Kensley before returning her attention to the ice.

Tucker slams Luca into the boards, and I wince, feeling his pain. It was a dirty maneuver, but they were both chasing the puck.

"Who says we've hooked up?" Kensley glares at me as if I'm the one that's been gossiping about my best friend.

"It wasn't me."

Zeke tries removing his headphones, and I plant my hands on both of his ears, reminding him it stays on.

"I've seen you all over Brooks at the aftergame parties. Come on. Are you two not hooking up?" Nova's waiting for an explanation.

"We're dating, but we're taking things slow," Kensley says, and her cheeks redden. "Not that it's anyone's business."

"Fair enough." Nova smiles at Kensley. "I'm just glad you and Brooks are dating. I swear he's had a crush on you since you first showed up at a party with Harper."

"I'm not sure he even noticed me that first time, but we did get to talking and hanging out. He's cute and, yeah, that's all I'm going to say about it." Kensley's face is as red as a tomato.

I've never seen her flustered.

It's actually quite cute and quite clear to me that she really likes Brooks. I'm glad she's found someone to keep her busy. I feel a bit like a shitty friend for not being around and hanging out with her as much as I'd like, but it's hard, between Zeke and classes.

Luca hits the puck to Liam, and it slices past the goalie, landing right into the net.

We're on our feet, cheering and screaming as the Narwhals take the lead in the third period.

It's a close game, Luca shoving Black out of the way as he races for the puck and is slammed into the plexiglass by Tucker.

I curse under my breath.

Luca shakes it off and gets back out there like nothing just happened. It amazes me how he can focus again, and he does, so quickly.

The other team gets close to our goal and Brooks deflects the puck, knocking it toward Liam on the right. Liam manages to touch the puck with his stick, and within half a second, he gets checked into the boards and bounces off them, the puck skittering across the ice with him.

I imagine he's cursing and pissed, but Liam is back chasing right after the puck and shooting it toward Luca, who knocks it right past their goalie. Their teamwork is impeccable and so much more graceful than the Predators. It should be no surprise they win, but I imagine it still feels really good to the team.

After the game, we head toward the locker room, waiting outside for them to finish getting showered and dressed.

Zeke won't sit still, and while I know he's probably overtired, I let him run around the hallway, making sure that he doesn't get too far from my reach.

There's been no sign of that strange man with the snake tattoo. Thankfully, he hasn't seemed to follow us to Great Falls.

Liam and Brooks step out of the locker room first, carrying their duffel bags.

"Liam!" Zeke shrieks with giggles and runs right for Liam.

Liam drops his bag and bends down, arms open, giving Zeke a huge hug. "Hey, buddy, I like your jersey. Did you wear that just for me?"

"No!" Zeke giggles and tugs on the hem of the oversized jersey, pulling back slightly. "For Daddy."

Playfully, Liam pouts and hangs his head. "You didn't wear it for me?"

Zeke tackles Liam with a giant hug.

Liam swoops the little guy off the ground and lifts him into the air. "Are you going to play hockey like your old man?" he asks.

Zeke wiggles to be put down and Liam hands him off to me as the locker room door swings open.

"Daddy!" Zeke shouts and points at Luca as he steps out of the locker room with Ashton.

"You guys did great today!" I say, congratulating them on their win.

Liam picks up his bag, and he and Brooks move out of the way as Luca offers to take Zeke from me. "It helped to have our favorite people in the stands," Luca says.

"Is that me?" Zeke asks, a huge smile on his face.

"You and your mother," Luca says, giving me a wink. Luca turns his attention entirely on me. "How do you feel about going out with us and celebrating before we drive home?"

"We have Zeke," I say, glancing at my little dragon and ruffling his hair. "It has to be someplace that he's allowed inside."

"No, we'll make him stand outside in the cold," Luca jokes and rolls his eyes. He nudges me. "You should know me better than that."

He drops a kiss on my cheek.

I've missed going out with the guys and having fun. I don't know how that's going to happen with a three-year-old in the mix.

"What do you say, Harper?" Liam asks. "Join us for a night of karaoke and non-alcoholic drinks?"

I snort. Even if they wanted to drink, most of them are underage.

"What about your coach? Don't you have to head back to campus tonight?" I ask.

"We convinced him it would be a good opportunity to celebrate and do some team-building," Ashton says. There's a smirk on his face.

Clearly, Coach fell for it.

I don't see these guys doing any team-building exercises tonight.

Just having fun on the town.

"I'm in if you're in," I say, staring at Luca.

"Let's go!"

We make our way to the small-town restaurant that features karaoke on Friday nights. Since it's a restaurant, it's open to all ages, and we manage to snag a table and put in an order for some appetizers to share.

"Who's singing first?" Liam asks as he pulls up an extra chair and straddles it, sitting backward. He rests his arms on the back of the chair, his chin resting on his hands.

"Go for it," I say, gesturing for him to take the lead.

"You don't want to hear me sing." Liam grins. "You'll be paying me to get off the stage."

There's already someone up at the microphone singing a rendition of a familiar '90s song that I recognize but don't quite know all the lyrics.

"Does anyone want to do a duet?" Nova asks.

"I'll sing with you," Kensley offers. "What songs do they have?"

"There's an app you can use to browse the karaoke catalog." Liam gives us the information and Nova grabs her phone, typing it in and downloading the app.

After a few minutes of everyone deciding what to sing, Liam, Nova, Kensley, Brooks, and a few others start making their way up to put their name and song choice down.

"You're not going to go up there?" Luca asks, watching me with a smile.

"Have you heard me sing? No one wants to hear that." I shake my head adamantly. "I'm here to support everyone else. What about you?"

"I'd rather go hang out with Dante than sing in front of my friends."

Liam is the first back from putting his name down on the sheet. "Will you take a picture of me up there with my phone?"

"Yeah, of course."

"Thanks." He scrolls through his social media feed and studies his phone for way too long. I catch a glimpse, and I'm pretty sure he's looking at photos of the girl he had over a couple of months ago.

I can't quite remember her name, but she was cute.

Liam never brought her to the house again. He also hasn't mentioned her and, well, it's none of my business. I assume it just didn't work out between them.

A few minutes later, Liam is called up to the stage, and he shoves his phone at me. The screen flickers for a second and goes dark.

Shit.

Liam grabs the microphone and smiles at everyone. "Just remember, I play hockey better than I sing."

The group chuckles at his remark as the music begins.

Liam doesn't have a terrible voice. It's not the perfect song choice that he went with, a little too high a key, but he makes it work. The more comfortable he gets out there, he sounds even better.

Perhaps it was his nerves making him sound a little rough in the beginning.

Shit.

I still haven't gotten a photo of him yet.

He has way too many apps on his phone and I swipe up, finding dozens of apps open. I open the camera one and hit the button.

Turns out, I'm video recording the whole thing.

Oops.

I glance down, realizing it shows as live and quickly end the video.

Sorry, Liam. Please don't hate me.

Hopefully, no one saw the live feed. I click on the camera and snap a couple of photos, trying to make up for the blunder.

No one ever has to know.

Liam finishes and comes back to the table, a huge grin on his face.

"You did amazing!" I hand him back his phone.

"Yeah? Thanks." He smiles sheepishly and glances through the karaoke app for another tune.

"Are you going to get up there?" Liam asks, glancing at me. "Come on. If I can do it, you can."

"I'll sing if Luca sings with me." I smirk at Luca; he groans and hangs his head.

"Don't make me get on stage."

"Do you have stage fright?" I ask, curious why he's so adamant about not singing.

Our waitress brings the appetizers, and Zeke grows restless, reaching for one of the fried pickles.

"You have to let it cool off. The inside is going to be hot." I put a couple aside for him and then when he grows fussy, I cut them in half, letting it cool a little quicker before sliding the plate in front of him.

"I don't have stage fright. I'd just rather play babysitter to my son all night. Someone has to watch him. We both can't be on stage at the same time." Luca has an excuse for everything.

It's not like it's just the three of us at the restaurant doing karaoke. Our roommates and friends are here. I'm sure they'd take a turn for a few minutes keeping an eye on Zeke.

"Oh, I reached out to my father this evening on the way to the game."

That catches me by surprise. Luca rarely talks to his father unless he absolutely has to contact him. "You did?"

"I thought I'd mention the man with the snake tattoo. Turns out, he's the son of Massimo DeLuca."

"Who is that?" I ask.

Luca sighs and runs a hand through his hair. He grabs a pretzel bite and dips it into the honey mustard sauce, taking a bite.

I'm waiting for him to answer.

He seems to be avoiding finishing our conversation.

"Luca?"

"He's a problem," Luca says, glancing up at me.

Frustration singes through my veins. "I thought we weren't keeping secrets anymore?" How can he tell me this guy is a problem and then not say anything else.

"We're not. I'm telling you, *he's a problem.*"

Why is Luca always so fricking cryptic when it comes to his father's business dealings? "How big of a problem are we talking, Luca? Like something that will get buried under the rug and go away, or is this guy going to be a threat until he's taken care of—"

He lowers his voice. "The second option."

Fuck.

"Why us?" I ask, wanting more answers than he's provided. "Why is he after my son?"

Luca scoots closer, his breath against my ear. "This is not a conversation we should be having out in public."

I laugh under my breath. "Well, if you'd had it with me at home this evening, we wouldn't be doing this now, would we?"

He rolls his lips together and exhales loudly through his nose. "Like I said, I texted Dante on the way to the game." He's growing irritated with me. He grabs another bite of pretzel and stuffs it into his mouth.

My shoulders deflate.

That's right.

He didn't know earlier.

I can't blame him for not telling me something that he didn't know.

"We'll figure it out." I reach for his hand, giving it a squeeze before glancing down at my phone. Maybe I can convince Nova or Kensley to go up there and sing with them?

"Liam Moretti!" a female voice shouts across the restaurant as she storms inside, and I can't help but glance up at the brunette.

She's the same girl Liam invited over months ago.

Except this time, she's definitely not looking happy to see him.

Liam shifts uncomfortably in his chair. I would be, too, if someone were staring at me like they wanted my death served right up.

"What are you doing here?" Liam asks, and I can't help but watch the exchange. It's far more interesting than picking out a song.

"If you didn't want me to find you, maybe don't post a live with you doing karaoke," she snaps back.

Liam turns and glares at me. "Harper? What the hell?"

FOURTEEN

LIAM

Bristol Greyson is the last person I expect to find joining us tonight—although I'm not sure she's technically joining us. It seems like she showed up to give me a tongue lashing.

Typical of Bristol.

I can't believe Harper made a video and put it out for everyone to see on social media! Was she trying to humiliate me?

"Seriously, Harper?"

"Sorry," she grimaces and her cheeks blush, "the phone glitched, and then I was trying to find the camera feature, and you have a lot of apps on your phone. I screwed up."

"Yes, you did," I grumble, annoyed.

Luca scoots his chair between Harper and me. "If you have a problem with my wife, take it up with me, Liam."

"Stay out of it, Ricci." Why does he have to fight all of his wife's battles? I turn around, facing Bristol and ignoring Luca, which I'm not sure is the better option.

"What do you want, Firebreather?" I snap, glancing her over.

She's dressed up, sort of. Bristol is wearing a Predators' jersey—she's clearly the enemy—and black, skin-tight leggings, which show off her thighs. But the dressed-up bit is the dark-green, sparkly heels, and her hair and makeup look freshly done.

"Cute shoes." I glance down at the sparkly shoes that seem a little too dressy for the outfit.

Her eyes widen in horror as she glances down at her feet.

“Oh my gosh!” Red creeps onto her cheeks and she slinks into the nearest chair at our table.

“I didn’t say that you could join us,” I grumble at Bristol.

“Yeah, well, fuck off, Moretti. I’m sitting.” She folds her hands on the table and glares at me.

Is this a staring contest?

I’m pretty sure I’d win.

But if it’s a silent competition, she loses, because she opens her mouth first. “I didn’t say you could call my father, twice. Now, look where we are.” She glares at me.

“You called her father?” Luca’s voice catches in his throat. “Kyler Greyson?”

“He owes me a favor,” I boast. I refrain from pointing out that I technically only called Kyler once, the other time I texted him. He, however, called me.

“I owe you something, Moretti. How about a black eye?” Bristol threatens, showing her rage in the form of a fist.

"Liam," the DJ announces my name to sing the next song. I stand and grab Bristol's arm.

"You're coming with me."

"What?" Her eyes widen in horror. "You're not serious!"

I drag her with me up on stage, and the DJ hands me a microphone and then her one as well.

"You're an asshole," Bristol grumbles at me.

I offer a wry grin. "Thanks, Firebreather."

The song "Gives you Hell" begins playing.

Her mouth drops, and she glares at me with a wicked smile on her face.

It turns out, she knows the song by the All-American Rejects. She doesn't even look at the screen displaying the lyrics as she pins me with her stare, singing the lyrics right to me.

As she starts the chorus, an angry smile breaks on her face. Bristol continues singing, dancing to the beat of the music, putting on quite the entertaining show.

Her hips sway, and my body can't not react to her proximity and movements.

I try to keep up at least in terms of singing, my tone matching hers as we harmonize together, which only seems to anger her further.

I can't seem to catch a break.

During the brief instrumental break, she flips me off. By the end, she's practically sing-screaming at me as she's staring me dead in the eyes.

I'm waiting for a mic-drop at the end, and so is the DJ because he carefully holds out his hand for the microphone.

Bristol forces a smile at him and hands him the microphone. She flips me off again, glaring at me as she saunters off the stage in those ridiculous sparkly heels.

I don't dare admit that her little performance turned me the fuck on.

And those glittery shoes, yeah, she can leave those on and nothing else in my next fantasy.

"You're still an asshole, Moretti," she barks at me and saunters over to the bar area.

I follow after her, even though I should probably give the witch some space.

She leans on the bar, gesturing for the bartender.

"What can I get for you?" he asks.

"Sex on the Beach," Bristol says.

"I'm going to need to see your I.D."

She reaches into her purse and hands him what has to be a fake I.D. because I know she's not twenty-one.

He glances it over, checks the date of birth, and hands it back. "Anything for you?"

"No, I'm good."

I lean closer, my lips brushing against her ear, so only she can hear me. "So, you're twenty-one now?" I ask, skeptical. She's in her sophomore year, same as I am.

She shifts around to face me, folding her arms across her chest. There's a warning written across her face, not to cross her.

"So, how are you?" I force a smile, trying to break the obvious tension hanging in the air between us.

"Better, now that I showed you up on stage."

"You certainly outdanced me." I admit defeat in that category. I wasn't moving my hips. I barely moved at all while I sang, because, quite frankly, it took too much energy to remember to open my mouth and let the music come out, while she was doing that hip sway thing and staring straight into my soul.

She leaves her credit card with the bartender, then takes her drink, walking back to the table with my friends and teammates.

Damn, the girl has some nerve.

I'm right on her heels, heading for my chair when she snatches it first.

I grab another chair from a nearby table, scooting it over and boldly sit next to her. She raises an eyebrow at me as she sips her liquor.

"We met briefly before," Harper says, and holds out her hand, introducing herself. "I'm Harper Ricci."

"Bristol," she says and offers her hand. "Yeah, I remember the little man, is it Zeke?"

"It is," Harper says.

Zeke beams and climbs from Harper's lap and over to Bristol.

"It seems he remembers you too." Harper laughs, amused by her son's antics.

"Hey, do you want to sit with me?" Bristol asks, and Zeke climbs onto her lap. She keeps her drink out of his reach as he keeps extending his arm out, wanting to grab it.

"If he's bothering you—"

"Oh, it's no bother. He's cute. Sweet even. Unlike this ogre," Bristol says and jabs her thumb in my direction.

"Ogre?" I glare at her. "I'm surprised you know such a big word."

"I know a lot of big words, most of them aren't appropriate for Zeke." Bristol's icy gaze sends a chill down my spine.

Zeke keeps reaching for Bristol's drink, and as she takes a long sip, his hand dunks into the colorful concoction. I grab his hand and a napkin, wiping him clean and taking him from Bristol so she can finish her drink without anyone wearing it.

Bristol finishes her drink and heads for the bar, ordering another while I watch her, mesmerized by the enemy.

She's spellbinding, but I can't quite figure out why.

"You like her," Luca says, watching my gaze and following it. "Somehow, I doubt that she feels the same way."

"You're wrong." Harper smacks Luca's arm. "He definitely has a shot with her; he just has to take it."

"No, I think Luca's right on this one. Bristol and I have hated each other since the first grade." I'm not about to recant the story to them, but the tension they feel, it's not unresolved sexual tension; it's pure hatred.

Zeke wiggles off my lap and runs across the restaurant and toward the bar, making a beeline straight for Bristol.

"I'll get him," I offer, hurrying toward the bar.

"Hey," Bristol says and bends down, scooping Zeke into her arms. "I'll bet it's past your bedtime." She glances over her shoulder, noticing me, but doesn't say anything.

"No bedtime," Zeke proclaims. "Want." He points at the drink that the bartender is making Bristol.

"Sorry, Zeke, that's not for you," I say. "Do you want me to take him?"

"Would you? Wrestling him and heels are a lethal combination." Bristol smiles at me, and it's as natural as the sun setting. My heart leaps in my chest.

It's probably the alcohol making her giddy but damn, I'm not complaining.

I don't count how much Bristol has to drink. She goes to the bar a few more times before Coach, who is sitting at another table, gives us a ten-minute warning.

We wrap up, pay the bill, and have to head back to the bus.

Bristol stumbles as she walks on those sparkly heels and giggles as I catch her, my hands instantly wrapped around her hips. "Are you always going to be my hero?" She smiles up at me.

It's a sight that I never imagined witnessing in all of my life.

Bristol Greyson is drunk.

And she's a happy drunk.

"How'd you get here?" I ask, glancing her over. She's not in any condition to drive home, not that I believe she has a car, at least she didn't the last time we caught up together.

"The bus," she slurs, and I glance at my watch. I'm concerned about her taking the bus, alone, at this hour, while in her current inebriated condition.

"Harper, can you watch her for a minute?" I ask and hurry off to find our coach.

"I don't need watching!" Bristol hollers back and smiles at Harper. "Your son is *so* adorable."

I jog toward Coach, who is getting all the players back onto the bus, taking an inventory of us to make sure that no one gets left behind. "I can't in good conscience let Bristol take the bus home alone. She's drunk, and I'd feel terrible if something happened to her—"

"What are you suggesting, Moretti?" Coach glares at me. "This isn't a party bus. We're not giving free rides out or taking girls home."

"Of course not," I say. "I'll make sure she gets home, and then I'll take the city bus back to campus."

Coach's eyes tighten and he nods. "You're a good kid. Do you have enough money to get back to EU?"

I tap my wallet, making sure it's in my pants pocket. "Yes, sir."

"We'll take your equipment back to campus." He's referring to my duffel bag already on the bus. The team always handles our hockey equipment for us.

"Thanks, Coach."

He pats me on the shoulder, his grip firm as he holds my forearm. "Make smart decisions, Moretti."

"Always."

I hurry back toward Bristol, who is chatting up a storm with Harper.

"I'm taking you home," I say to Bristol, throwing an arm around her shoulder.

Bristol glances me up and down and then looks at the bare parking lot. "You don't have a car."

She's right, my car is back at home. "We'll take the bus. That's how you got here, isn't it?"

"I hitchhiked." She grins at me, and I swear she'd better be joking, or I'm about to give her a twenty-minute lecture on safety.

"You did not," I growl between clenched teeth and escort her toward the bus stop across the street.

"I'm kidding," she says, and leans against me. My arm instantly falls around her hip, holding her to me, keeping her upright and steady.

Luca chases after me. "Where are you two off to?"

"I'm going to make sure she gets home safely."

"Do you want me to give you a ride? I can swing back after and pick up the girls." Luca glances back at the vehicle where everyone is waiting to be let in.

There are too many of us to all fit into his vehicle in one shot. "It's not a big deal. She lives on campus; it's like ten minutes from here by bus."

"Who knows when the next bus comes through here at this hour? I'll drive you both to campus."

The girls grumble as they head back inside the restaurant to stay warm. Thankfully, they're still open for a while longer.

I help Bristol into the front seat while I climb in back.

"Fun night?" Luca asks as he glances at Bristol.

"The Predators lost. So, no. Not fun for me." She shuffles into the seat, secures her seatbelt, and I give Luca directions to her dorm.

He doesn't ask how I know where she lives or what building she's in.

When we finally arrive, I climb out of the car, helping her to her feet.

"I'll wait for you."

"Don't," I tell him. "I'll catch the city bus back home."

"Seriously?" Luca shakes his head. "She's drunk, Liam."

I shove my face back into the car, glaring at Luca. "I'm well aware. She's also fainted on me too many times over the summer. I'm not taking a chance that something happens to her or someone takes advantage of her. I know to be a gentleman." I slam the door shut, and Bristol is already a few feet ahead of me, walking herself home.

I'm right beside her, strolling up, my arm around her waist while I glance over my shoulder as Luca pulls away.

"You don't have to walk me home. Wait. How are you going to get home?" she mumbles, her words slur together.

"I'll figure it out later."

The answer is the bus, but I don't need to tell her that right now.

She slips her arm around my waist and pulls me against her chest, cuddling me.

Instantly, my arms envelop her, and I can feel her breath against my racing heart. "It's cold, we should go inside."

It's not that cold for early October, but I'm grateful to keep moving and walk her inside the building.

Bristol could use a glass of water and a bed, to sleep off the alcohol.

"Inside," she says and smiles up at me. "Okay. Good idea."

I escort her inside and up to the elevator. I'm constantly at her hip, worried she'll pass out on me, but she doesn't faint.

She stays completely upright, except that she stumbles in those heels every so often. I keep her from tripping and falling, my arm practically a natural extension of her body, holding her against me.

I don't dare admit that it feels good.

The elevator dings as we arrive at her floor and I follow her out, letting her lead the way.

She's on the same floor but in a different room this time. Apparently, she's moved dorms since the last time we met.

Good information for me to have.

Bristol fiddles with her keys, struggling to get it into the lock.

"Here, let me," I say, wrapping my hand around hers as I steady her trembling hand.

The key slides in, turns and she opens the door, showing me her dorm room.

There's a single twin bed in the room, a desk at the opposite wall.

The walls are plastered in posters and rope lights that are currently on. It gives off a nice mood lighting and a bit of a witchy feel with her crystal ball on the corner and her tarot cards lying next to it.

"No roommate?" I ask.

"Not this year."

There's an array of fancy clothes, including that short leather skirt, strewn across her mattress. I wish she'd worn that sexy ensemble tonight, instead of the Predators' jersey, but Bristol would intentionally wear the one thing that would piss me off—the opposing team's jersey.

She shoves the clothes to the floor in a heap.

"I never took you to be messy." I tilt my head, curious what's going through her mind.

"I couldn't decide what to wear tonight." She plops down on the bed and wiggles her feet at me. "I forgot I put these killers on."

I bend down, helping Bristol out of her heels, placing them on the floor. "You should climb under the covers, get some sleep."

"Are you going to join me?" Bristol grins and lifts her hips, sliding her leggings down, revealing a glimpse of skin.

I glance away, not because I want to, but because it feels like the right thing to do.

She's drunk or, at the very least, tipsy.

I am not taking advantage of her.

Even if she throws herself at me.

Even if Bristol begs me to fuck her.

I won't.

"That's not a very good idea," I say and clear my throat, the sound betraying me as it catches and sounds raspy.

Bristol is sexy as hell when she's only wearing a jersey.

Too bad it's not my jersey.

"Why do you have to wear that monstrosity?" I grumble, glaring at the Predators written across her chest.

"You don't like it?" Bristol points at her chest. "Maybe you like what's underneath?"

She lifts the hem of her jersey, and in one swift movement, it's on the floor.

Her breasts are perky and gorgeous.

She isn't even wearing a bra. The only layer of clothing nestled against her are the dark-ruby panties that are lace and see-through.

My cock twitches in my pants.

Now is not the time to get a hard-on for Bristol Greyson.

Never is about the right time, but I'm not doing something she'll regret come morning and have the police at my door, labeling *me* a predator.

I spin around, doing everything I can to not stare at her gorgeous breasts or the perfect complexion of her skin, how she looks like an absolute goddess.

She's the enemy.

The reminder doesn't help my cock. It doesn't seem to care who she is, only how sexy she looks right now.

I stalk across the room to her dresser, stumbling through the drawers, finding an oversized t-shirt and tossing it at her. "Put that on," I grunt.

I swear I can hear the pout in her voice. "Do I have to?"

"Yes." I exhale heavily and fold my arms across my chest. I run a hand through my hair. "Are you decent yet?"

"I'm always decent," Bristol says, and I chance a glance over my shoulder as she's wearing the t-shirt.

She slips under the covers, still sitting up in bed. "Are you sure you don't want to join me?" Her hands wrestle under the blankets, and I give her a curious expression when she tosses those bare-thin red lace panties straight at my face.

I'm not expecting them or the fact that she's half-naked in bed.

"You really don't like me, do you?" Her bottom lip juts out in a pout, and I bite down on my own lip to avoid striding across the room and kissing her.

"I hate you."

It's a little white lie.

I have to say it so I can compel myself not to fall for Bristol and her vixen ways.

"I hate you too," she says, but she doesn't sound convincing. "We can hate fuck." Bristol grins at me as she lies back on the bed. "I'll wear whatever you want. Even my ex-boyfriend's t-shirt," she gestures to the shirt she's in, "if that gets you off."

I toss my head back and stare up at the ceiling.

Perhaps I should have left well enough alone. Let her take the bus home and gone back with the team.

Because Bristol, at this rate, will have me murdered by her father if he gets wind of any of this. Even if I don't sleep with her, this whole scenario could get me sanctioned and kicked off the team.

“I should go.” I stumble back toward the door.

“Wait!” Bristol’s eyes widen, and she sits up in bed. “You’re actually going to leave me like this?” Her face flushes with what I can only assume is embarrassment.

I stand with the door to my back, just inches from escape.

“Of course, you hate me.” She’s spiraling. “You’ve always hated me and I stupidly throw myself at you because that’s what I do when I like someone.” She slams her eyes shut and is berating herself.

Sighing, I step forward toward the bed and grab her desk chair, pulling it over to sit beside her. “You’ve been drinking, Bristol. Nothing can happen until you’re sober. When you can actually give consent. Right now, it would be me taking advantage of you.”

Her brow pinches.

“I’m not drunk.”

“You’re not sober, either,” I counter. I’d bet she’s more than just a little tipsy, with the way she was throwing those panties at me, but I’ll let it slide.

"How about you lie back down, close your eyes, and get some sleep? I'll stay until you fall asleep."

"I'm not tired."

Me neither, not when Bristol is throwing herself at me.

Even if I wanted to fuck her, tonight is not the night.

"Then talk to me until you fall asleep."

She grumbles and lies back down, resting her head on the pillow. Bristol shifts onto her side, pulling the blankets up but staring at me. "Talk about what?" She fights a yawn, just like Zeke would when Luca tells him it's bedtime.

"You did good tonight singing, dancing up on stage. No fainting," I say, a bit surprised she managed to last an entire night without an episode.

"Yeah," she nods slowly, "I'm on medicine now." Bristol yawns. "Ariella's doctor was amazing. I mean, after she ran a bazillion different tests and practically tortured me as part of her practicing medicine."

"Amazing, huh?" I stare down at Bristol. "I think you and I have different definitions of amazing. Not that the sound of Bristol Greyson being tortured is terrible." I crack a grin, and she snarls at me and shows her fist.

I grab it, keeping her from landing a blow on me. "You're a jerk."

"I know. I thought we already established that you love to hate me."

Bristol rolls onto her back. "You might be onto something." Her eyes flutter closed.

"Are you going to tell me about that medical condition?" I ask curiously.

"Buzz off." She throws up her middle finger at me before ignoring me and drifting off to sleep.

I stay through the night, wanting to be there if she has a problem.

I fall asleep uncomfortably on the chair.

"Liam?" Bristol's voice rattles me awake.

My eyes flash open and the crick in my neck is unbearable. It's also still dark outside.

"Go back to sleep." I force a smile and shift on the chair, my legs stretched out beneath the bed.

Bristol pulls back the covers and shifts on the mattress, her back flush against the wall. “Join me.”

“Do you really think that’s a good idea?”

“Just sleep,” she grumbles at me. “I’m not offering you anything more.”

I slip out of my shoes and climb under the covers with her. The bed is toasty, and I roll onto my side, trying to give us both ample space on the twin mattress.

Stretching out helps my neck, and I shut my eyes, trying to sleep.

The bed shifts as Bristol seems to grow restless. My back is to her as I try desperately to ignore her subtle movements, which become more pronounced every few minutes.

“Am I taking up too much space?” I roll around to face her.

Bristol’s eyes are wide open.

Wordlessly, she shakes her head, and I let my eyelids flutter shut.

I’m exhausted.

Hockey and Bristol will do that to me.

“Sleep.” I pull her against me.

Her body is tense and I let my fingers caress over her back and down just above her ass. She hums softly and sighs, curling up against me, sliding her leg between mine.

“Goodnight,” I whisper, kissing her cheek before I’m out cold.

FIFTEEN

BRISTOL

How does he manage to fall asleep while rubbing my back? His fingers graze my ass, and it takes everything in my power not to jump his bones.

Holy hell, the proximity, his scent, my body feels like it's in heat.

Damn hormones.

I can't remember the last time I was so turned on by a guy, let alone one I hated. Definitely not my ex-boyfriend. Not that I hated him. When we dated, I was into him, but he never turned me on like this, just being close to him.

It could be the fact Liam and I have so much pent-up, unresolved sexual tension that it's mounting like a volcano ready to erupt.

Well, there's always something ready to blow up between us, not usually sexual in nature.

Pressed up against him, my leg slides between his. I need to feel his warmth, his comfort. It settles my racing heart, which I can't explain.

The racing heart, I understand, it's his touch that soothes me I find oddly satisfying and without reason.

He's an enigma, Liam Moretti.

I should hate him.

I do hate him, on most days.

Last night, he was sweet, bringing me back home, making sure I got to my dorm safe, and then staying with me.

I would have expected a hockey player like Liam to attempt taking advantage of a drunk girl. Yes, I had too much to drink. Anything over one drink, and I'm always tipsy. It doesn't help that I don't drink that often.

My fingers slide under his t-shirt, my palms pressed up against his warm skin as he sleeps.

Liam curls against me, rolling and pinning me on my back.

Fuck, yes.

A girl can fantasize and dream.

I let his warmth, his body, lull me to the perfect dreamland. I don't know how long I'm asleep, but I feel quite refreshed and definitely sober when my eyelids flutter open.

There's a hint of sunlight peeking through the curtains as the sun begins to rise.

Liam still has me pinned on my back, his body half covering mine, his hand on my hip and his breath nestled in my neck.

Fuck, I'm turned on right now.

He's asleep, but his cock seems to have other ideas as it begins stirring.

Is it our proximity, or is he dreaming something hot and sexy in his sleep?

He grumbles, a typical Liam sound. Asleep or not, he makes the same dissatisfied noises around me all the time.

I chalk it up to annoyance.

He grinds his hips against me, and holy hell, I'm sure as fuck he's having a sex dream because his cock is pressed against me, and it's hard.

I'm not wearing panties and I try to roll away, but I smack into the wall and groan.

Liam's eyes flash open and it seems to take him a second to register where he is.

"Bristol?" He glances at me, confused, and then pulls back, taking much of the covers with him.

I shiver and yank the blankets back over my body. "Quit being a blanket hog."

He rolls over, his back to me, probably trying to hide his morning wood he's sporting.

Too late, Moretti, I already felt it between my legs, and damn, was it big.

Too bad he hadn't nudged it a little higher and closer up my thigh.

He coughs and rubs at his hair, sitting up, his back to me. He glances at his watch, like he has somewhere to be at this hour. It's Saturday.

"That was quite a dream you were having," I whisper.

Liam clears his throat. "Was it? I don't remember any of it." He pushes more blankets back around me as a truce and adjusts himself.

"Do you remember waking up, pinning me to the bed with your body?" I whisper, daring him to turn and look at me.

His shoulders tense. "I didn't realize what was happening. I'm sorry." Liam hangs his head and grabs his shoes, quickly putting them back on.

I sit up beside him. My hand goes to his shoulder, trying to get him to look at me. The smile on my face won't disappear, no matter how much I want it to right now. "Liam, look at me."

Sighing, he glances back at me over his shoulder, and I lean up on my knees, capturing his mouth with mine. Within seconds, I'm climbing onto his lap, straddling him.

Surprise is evident when he fumbles backward, his legs dangling off the edge of the bed, and I pull back, laughing. “Too much?”

I can feel his hard-on poking me, and it takes everything in my power not to glide my hand down the waistband of his pants.

Liam stares up at me, breathless.

“Fuck, Bristol. I’m not sure I’m not still dreaming.”

I bring my hands down and pin his arms playfully to the bed. “You’re wide awake, and you’re mine.” I lean down, hovering over his lips, teasing him.

He raises up, against my body, our chests pressed together as he captures my lips and unbinds his hands from my grip, wrapping them around my waist.

Liam rolls us around, putting me on my back as he climbs up my torso. One hand dances across my thighs and over my bare hip. He’s skirting where I most want him to touch me.

“Wait.” I press a hand to his chest, stopping him.

Liam’s breath is ragged, and he pulls back, climbing off my body like I’ve burned him.

"I just ... I need to take my medicine before we do anything like this," I gesture between us. "And, umm, we need a condom too."

Liam comes prepared, whipping out his wallet and showing me what he's packing.

I'm not sure if I should feel relieved or mortified. Has he thought about this with me a lot, or does he pack condoms in case he runs into a girl he wants to sleep with?

Best not to ask.

I really don't want to hear the answer.

"Where are your pills?" Liam asks, moving off the mattress.

"On the desk." I point to the desk and the colorful pillbox where my medications are stored for the week.

He brings me the container along with a bottle of juice from the fridge.

"Thanks," I say, snapping the lid of the pills and pouring them into my palm.

His eyes widen, surprised by the number of prescriptions that I'm taking. "Don't judge me." I glare at him.

"Wouldn't dream of it. If the pills are helping..." he trails off when his phone buzzes, and he checks it briefly while I take medication with orange juice.

"Everything okay?" I ask.

He holds out his hand for the empty pill container, and I offer it to him to put back on my desk.

"Just Luca, making sure I'm all right since I never made it home last night."

Luca checking up on Liam is next level. I never thought guys did that with each other.

I hand him the small bottle of juice, and he tucks it back into the fridge.

"That's nice. I didn't realize he was sweet on you," I tease him.

He tosses his middle finger up at me, but the smile on his face is playful and not at all mad.

Our banter will never cease between us. Liam sits at the edge of the bed, his attention on me. The mood feels dampened by my new normal routine. “How are you feeling?”

I exhale and force a smile, not wanting to worry him. “Mornings are sometimes rough.” I reach for his hand. “It’s nice to have you here with me. I really thought you were going to bail last night after I fell asleep.”

Liam stretches and runs a hand through his hair. “I didn’t want to leave you alone, but I thought if I told you that, you’d either kick me out or shout at me.”

He’s not wrong. That sounds like something I’d do. “You know me too well, Moretti.”

“Okay, Greyson.” He pats my leg. “What’s on the agenda this morning? Breakfast out together? How’s that hangover? Can you eat?”

“No hangover,” I say. I didn’t drink that much. I’m just a bit of a lightweight when it comes to consuming any alcohol.

I raise an eyebrow, sizing him up. “Are you suggesting that we go out together, on a date?”

“You call it the ‘d-word’ all you want. Doesn’t mean

I'm giving you that d." Liam winks at me. "I'm calling it breakfast."

"I wasn't asking for your dick!" I shoot back, smacking his arm.

"I'm beginning to notice a violent tendency in you, Bristol."

I snort. Seriously? He's noticing it *now*? "You're cute, but you're not very observant." I punched him when we were kids for being a jerk. Is it only now dawning on him? They say that boys take longer to mature, does it also take them longer to grow some brains and common sense?

"Not observant?" He takes pause and tilts his head, staring at me. "I've caught you from falling when you've fainted how many times?"

I point at him. "That's not fair. Anyone can notice that when your eyes roll back in your head."

He scoots back onto the bed, sitting beside me. "Is that what you think happens? That's a cute description, but you get more of a blank look on your face, like you just mentally checked out."

I stick my tongue out at Liam and he leans closer, his hand on my cheek, his mouth capturing mine, taking my tongue past his lips.

Holy hell, the kiss is fire and my body tingles in all the right ways.

One kiss is like stoking the fire, and I can't stop myself, nor do I want to when it comes to the way he makes me feel when his mouth is on mine.

He pulls me closer, lying on his side, his hand grazing my cheek and into my hair, caressing the nape of my neck. A shiver courses through me, and I tangle my legs with his, pulling him closer.

Liam's fingers move down to my ass, my shirt riding up slightly and his hand over my bare flesh sends tingles throughout my body.

Each kiss is more pronounced as he slowly backs off.

"Liam?" Already, I'm panting and gasping. My heart pounds wildly in my chest and the room spins as I try to catch my breath.

"How about we grab breakfast, and you spend the weekend with me?"

"Spend the weekend with you, here?" I ask. "Are you inviting yourself to stay in my dorm? That's ballsy, even for you."

Liam grins. "No, actually. I'm inviting you to come back with me to EU and stay at my house. It'll just be the girls tonight at the house, plus Zeke. I want you to get to know my friends and us to spend time together alone. Assuming we can do that and not kill each other." His lips linger over mine before he kisses me again.

"But I like threatening you with death." A smile spreads across my face. "In all seriousness, why do you want me to hang out with your friends?"

"My last partner was strictly friends-with-benefits. I'd like us to be more than just fuck buddies. Actual friends."

"You're asking a lot." I laugh. "And I didn't say I was going to sleep with you."

"Good, because I don't think you're ready for all this spice yet." Liam gestures at himself. "You might need to procure a doctor's note for what I've got planned."

My eyes widen and I smack his chest.

"You're too much!" I can't help but laugh as I rest my forehead against his shirt. Liam wraps his arms around me.

His embrace is strong and surprisingly comforting. "So, about that alone time at your house. When do you plan on that happening if I'm hanging out with your friends all weekend?"

"There's such a thing as nighttime, when people go to sleep." He's staring at me, trying not to laugh. "Besides, I have a bigger bed."

My eyes light up. "Oh."

"Sleep." He says again. "Stop thinking about my cock, dirty girl."

"I'm not thinking about your cock." My voice catches in my throat. At least I wasn't until he mentioned it. My gaze moves down between us, and I swear I feel his member twitch. Probably my imagination, because he's not sporting that massive boner like he had been when we first woke.

"Sure, you're not." The wry grin sends a shiver right through me. His gaze never wavers, forcing me to look away first.

"Who's to say I'm even going to have sex with you? We could just share a bed. Sleep." I diligently fold my arms across my chest, and he smirks.

"I'd be okay with cuddling you again." His hands firmly plant on my hips, and I feel the butterflies go wild inside me.

How does the man, whom I've hated all my life, have the ability to make my insides warm and toasty? One kiss, and I'm craving a lifetime more.

It doesn't make sense, but I nod and lean in, brushing my lips against his.

"But in all seriousness, Bristol, if you get sick of me and decide we're not worth one weekend together, I won't be mad. You can call it off at any time. I'll buy you a bus ticket or drive you back here. Whatever you want."

One weekend, to figure out whether we can survive liking each other or will kill one another.

SIXTEEN

LIAM

We grab breakfast in town then ride the bus back to Evergreen University. I carry Bristol's backpack, which contains an overnight change of clothes and her medicine. I'm not sure what else she stuffed inside, but I swear it's like she's stuffed a bag of bricks in there, so she can to see how much weight I can carry.

When we reach town, I lug her pack over my shoulder and escort her off the bus. "This is our stop."

"I know." Bristol returns a look that tells me this isn't her first time on campus.

Obviously.

I ran into her in the coffee shop, but that was during the summer, months ago. She could have forgotten how to get to my campus.

Turns out, she knows her way around. She leads me off the bus and takes a hard right in the direction of my house.

I hurry to catch up with her, my arm slipping around her waist, giving me the opportunity to touch her, and I'm curious if she'll push me away.

She hasn't so far, but I'm sure if I give it enough time, the enemy within her will pounce at me.

"How do you think your friends are going to react when you do the walk of shame?" Bristol asks, nudging against me as we walk.

I'm not sure it's on purpose, her movements sway just a bit, like she can't quite keep on the pavement.

"I've got nothing to be ashamed of. Besides, it's not like we even had sex. I never so much as got to touch your breasts."

Bristol snorts. "You sound disappointed."

“I am.” I bat my eyelashes at her, and she wrinkles her nose.

“Maybe you’ll get lucky tonight.” Her eyes widen at the realization of her words. “I mean, maybe you’ll get to touch my breasts if you’re a good boy.”

“When am I not good?” I smirk and let my fingers dance across her hip.

She shivers and pulls away. “That tickles.”

“Bristol Greyson is ticklish.” I laugh, the excitement bubbling within me at the realization that the girl will squirm and laugh from a simple touch. Never in my wildest dreams did I expect to see uncontrollable laughter escape from that girl’s lips.

“Yes.” She narrows her eyes at me and stays just out of my reach. Bristol fumbles with her feet onto the grass, and my arm is right back around her waist, pulling her forcefully against me, keeping her upright so she doesn’t fall.

“If you tickle me, Moretti, I swear to God—”

“You’ll what?” The temptation is overwhelming, but I know how much Sophia hated being tickled as a kid, and Mom made it very clear that no means no.

But honestly, the idea is entertaining, and just threatening her with it is fun.

"I'll chop off your dick," she warns with an evil smirk.

"Villain Bristol has come out to play." I keep my gaze tight on her as she shrugs her shoulders.

"I'm making it clear. It's a hard no. That's one line you don't cross, Moretti."

"Understood."

We approach the house and I'm surprised that Luca's car is still parked out front. It seems he hasn't left yet.

I unlock the front door and lead Bristol inside.

"Liam!" Zeke comes barreling for me, and I put Bristol's bag down on the ground before lifting the little man into my arms.

"Hey, bud. How are you this morning?" I give him a huge hug then put him down as he stares up at Bristol.

"Hi." He smiles up at her and makes a kissy face at her.

"Well, hello again." Bristol bends down to his height. "Long time, no see." She gives him a hug before he hurries off, running through the house.

"Mama!" Zeke squeals excitedly as he goes tearing into their bedroom.

I hope for Harper and Luca's sake, they're fully clothed back there.

Ashton stalks around the corner of the house, rubbing his eyes. It looks like he just rolled out of bed. "Someone woke me," he grumbles, glaring playfully at Zeke.

Zeke giggles, his dimples more pronounced as he runs past Ashton. "Nova!" Zeke shouts, looking for his other friend.

"Seriously?" Ashton playfully glares at Zeke. "Not even a good morning? You go running to steal my girlfriend. I'll remember that later," he teasingly threatens.

"Morning," Bristol says to Ashton, "although it is technically afternoon."

"Noon isn't afternoon. It's noon," Ashton growls and rubs a hand over his face. "It's too early for this shit." He stumbles into the kitchen while I escort Bristol to my bedroom, bringing her bag with me.

Turns out, her sass isn't solely reserved for me.

I'm not sure if I'm jealous or relieved.

"Do I get a tour?" Bristol asks, following close behind me.

I flip on the bathroom light. "The bathroom." I wander past it to my room next door and let her inside. "My bedroom."

She glances around my room, taking it all in while I place her bag on my bed.

"Seriously, what did you pack, all your textbooks? A ton of bricks? A dead body?"

"Yes, Liam, I brought a dead body and stuffed it inside for you to dispose of. Thanks for getting your hands dirty." The witty smile adorns her face, and I refrain from kissing her.

It's not that I don't want to, I'm just never sure if she's going to cold cock me or kiss me back.

"Right. Well, deceased bodies go in the trash outside.

I can show you where that is if you'd like?" Two of us can play this game.

She snorts and plops down on my mattress beside her bag, lying back. "Your bed is so much bigger than mine." It's a full-sized bed. Not quite a queen, but it does offer enough room for two when I bring a girl over, which isn't often.

I haven't touched another girl since Iris, my friends-with-benefits who, well, we were hardly friends. Mostly, just benefits.

I want a girl to cuddle, to pull against me and whisper into her ear, watch her cheeks redden as I tell her all the naughty things I want to do to her, while her friends are oblivious to what I'm whispering.

"I'm glad you like it, because we're sharing my bed tonight." I smirk, hoping she doesn't decide to kick me to the couch, or worse, go home.

"We'll see," Bristol says and smiles. She sits up and glares at me. "What's on the agenda for today, *friendemy?*"

"Is that what you're going to call me from now on?" I'm amused by her antics. I crash next to her on the bed, our thighs bumping up together as my arm brushes hers. “And I think it’s frenemy,” I correct her.

“You would know.” She flashes a wicked grin and leans closer like she’s going to kiss me.

My breath catches in my throat, and I wait for her lips to descend on mine.

The heat, the spark, there’s sizzle in the air, the charge of electricity humming instinctively all around us.

Bristol pulls back, her blue eyes darkened like two sapphires as she glances at my lips. She clears her throat and stands, clearly flustered. “Agenda?” she asks again, but this time her cheeks are bright red.

I love the flush on her face, knowing it’s because she wants to kiss me.

“No agenda. Just a weekend of fun.” I reach for her hand, pulling her to sit beside me.

Her breathing is more pronounced, louder as she breathes entirely through her mouth, like she’s just run a marathon.

“You okay?” I ask, glancing her over.

Her hand is strangely cold, but her cheeks are a rosy red and sweat coats her forehead. I've seen this before, and I pull her to sit with me on the bed. "Don't go fainting on me, Firebreather."

"You've got to come up with a better nickname, Moretti." She rolls her eyes at me, but there's a hint of a smile playing at her lips, like she isn't quite mad.

"You're just jealous that you haven't come up with anything better than my last name."

Bristol shrugs.

She knows I'm right.

"How are you feeling?" I ask, staring at her, wanting her to be honest with me.

"I'll be okay." She forces a smile. "So, what do you guys do on the weekends around here?"

I refrain from telling her how Luca and Ashton typically spend the weekends up at Dante's compound, working for him.

"Whatever."

"Wow, you really know all the words, don't you?" she

mocks, and I stand, grabbing her hand, dragging her out to the living room.

“Liam, where are we going?”

“To play a game.” I lead her to the living room and put her on the couch. “I’ll be right back.”

“Okay.” She plops down on the sofa and glances around, taking everything in.

I head into the kitchen, where Ashton is making Nova and himself breakfast. “Are you and Luca heading to Dante’s this afternoon?” I’m surprised they haven’t left.

“We’re spending the weekend here. After what happened at the preschool, Luca isn’t comfortable leaving Harper and Zeke alone, and I tend to agree with him.”

“Who is Dante?” Bristol asks.

I glance up, seeing her standing on the other side of the breakfast bar. She grabs a seat at the bar, waiting for an answer.

So much for putting her on the sofa and having her wait there. Of course, she’s not Zeke, but it’s not as though he listens to me, either.

"Luca's father. They both work for him," Nova says, revealing far too much information than she should to Bristol.

What the hell, Nova?

"Oh, what does his father do?" Bristol asks, and there's a brief silence that fills the space.

Ashton grabs the orange juice container from the fridge, avoiding the question.

"He runs his own company. It's pretty boring work, logistics and shipping. They make you guys pack boxes and label stuff. Right?" I'm just making shit up at this point.

"Yeah, boring work," Ashton agrees rather quickly.

"Are you guys interested in a game this afternoon?" Bristol asks. She doesn't meet my stare, she's looking directly at Ashton and then Nova.

"Sure. What kind of game? Are you thinking cards, a board game? We've got some video games, too, in the living room," Nova asks.

Luca heads out of Zeke's bedroom, carrying the little guy with a fresh change of clothes. He heads into the bathroom, where our washer and dryer are stacked, with the laundry bin and spends a few minutes putting in a load.

We put on a movie and make a bowl of popcorn. Bristol curls up next to me on the couch and I dare admit I like when she puts her head on my shoulder, and I wrap my arms around her.

We skip lunch and order pizza for dinner. No one feels like cooking and the dining hall is a bit of a trek from the house.

"I still can't believe you like pineapple on pizza." I make a face at Bristol. "Super gross."

"It's not gross!" Nova chimes in, defending her. "It makes the flavor a million times better."

"A million times more gross," Ashton quips. "I'm with Liam. Nasty."

Nova rolls her eyes. "Fine, I won't kiss you with my pineapple pizza lips."

"Game night?" Harper asks as she packs up the last of the pizza and puts it in the fridge.

"Sure," Luca says. "Guest picks the game." Zeke has fallen asleep on the bean bag chair in the living room, and he picks him up and carries him to bed, putting him down for the night. The little guy must have been tuckered out.

Bristol's eyes widen. "That's me?"

I nod. "Take your pick, we've got all sorts of games in that cabinet." I gesture to the living room where there are board games stacked at the bottom and video games piled above it.

She saunters over and looks them thoroughly over. "Rapid Fire Questions?" Bristol asks.

"We don't have that one," Harper says.

"It's not an actual—"

"I know. I'm kidding." Harper plops down on the love seat, and Luca steals the spot next to her before anyone else can take it. "How long is each round? Thirty seconds, or a minute?"

Bristol grabs her spot on the sofa, and I'm right next to her.

"Thirty seconds. Who goes first?" I ask.

"Bristol, obviously, since she came up with the game." Harper gestures at Bristol. She grabs her phone. "I've got a timer we can use."

Ashton heads for the kitchen. “Where are you going?” I ask.

“This would be better as a drinking game,” he mutters and grabs a bottle of wine from the fridge. He unscrews the lid and brings the whole bottle with him.

“Are you planning on sharing that?” Nova stares at him from the floor. “Where are the cups?”

“I thought we could just drink out of the bottle. At least that’s my plan.” Ashton puts the bottle of wine in front of him and sits on the floor, pulling Nova onto his lap.

“You go first,” I remind Bristol.

“Right. Rapid Fire. Seeing as how there’s liquor, for every question someone chooses not to answer, they have to drink.”

“I thought you had to answer the questions. That’s the whole point of rapid fire.” Luca glances at Ashton. “You really don’t need the whole bottle of wine.”

“I might.” Ashton shrugs. “Besides, I’m willing to share. Bristol, are you ready?”

Harper hits the timer as the questions start flying out.

"Have you and Liam hooked up?" Harper asks.

"No," Bristol says.

"Do you have a crush on anyone?" Nova asks.

"Yes."

"Who?" I ask.

She glares at me and reaches for the bottle of wine.

I roll my eyes as she takes a swig.

"Last time you had sex?" Ashton asks.

I glare at him, but I am curious all the same.

"A year, maybe? I don't remember."

Well, she didn't opt to drink and hide that from everyone; that's something, I guess. "What's the medical condition you have?" I ask.

Her eyes widen, clearly surprised, and she shouts out a bunch of nonsense to me.

"POTS, EDS, MCAS."

Fuck if I know what those mean, but at least it's a starting point.

"That's time," Harper announces, and Bristol takes one more swig from the wine bottle. Her cheeks are flushed, and I can't help but stare at her.

"Your turn," Bristol says, staring at me.

"Shoot."

"Let me reset the timer," Harper says, and when she's ready, she points at me, for everyone to start firing their questions my way.

"When was the last time you had sex?" Bristol asks.

"Months, before our kiss." I stare at her. She could have just asked me, and I would have told her. Is that why she wanted to play this game?

"Any STIs?" she asks.

"None. I'm clean."

"Have you ever touched yourself and thought about me?" I reach for the liquor bottle in her hand. I'm pretty sure my non-committal is answer enough, but I'm not about to say as much in front of everyone.

I take a swig while Ashton fires up a question, getting one in while Bristol just asked three.

"Favorite sex position?" Ashton asks.

I snort, and my eyes widen. "Cowgirl."

The timer goes off, announcing the end of my turn.

Bristol wrinkles her nose. "That's too bad, because I'm more of a reverse cowgirl when it comes to sex positions."

My mouth drops and I take another swig, fighting the silence between us with alcohol.

Nova grins. "My turn. Do me next, but no sex questions. You guys are super pervy."

Harper starts the timer and rattles off the first question. "Do you work for your father or Luca's father?"

"No." The smile disappears from her face. "Why are you asking me that?"

"Spit or swallow?" Ashton asks.

She smacks his arm. "No sex questions, perv."

He laughs. "Fine. Do you want kids?"

"Yes. Eventually."

"Your major?" Bristol asks, giving her an easy one.

"Sociology."

"Your best friend?" I ask.

Nova glances between Ashton, Luca, and Harper. She grabs the alcohol bottle. "Don't make me choose."

The timer goes off. "Your turn." She points at Harper.

I get the distinct impression that Harper is Nova's best friend, but she values her relationship with both Ashton and Luca to not say as much. She doesn't want to hurt anyone's feelings. That's Nova, always putting others first.

Harper starts the timer. "Go!"

"Have you ever shot a gun?" Ashton asks.

"No."

"Ever buried a body?" I joke.

She gives me a peculiar look. "No. You're just wasting your questions."

"Are you keeping any secrets from me?" Luca asks, and runs his fingers through Harper's hair.

There have been a lot of secrets between them in the past, but she doesn't so much as hesitate. "No." She stares him in the eyes, and I know she wants to ask him the same question.

"Is Luca the biological father—"

"No," Harper answers before Bristol can finish the question.

"Did you two ever hook up during your study sessions?" I ask.

"No, we studied." Harper laughs and shakes her head.

"Have you ever had to fake it with that guy?" Ashton asks, pointing at Luca.

Luca growls at Ashton, and Harper rests a hand on his thigh. "No."

"I think you're lying," Ashton smirks. "You are always so loud, there's no way it's real."

"Oh, it's real. One hundred percent."

The timer buzzes, and Harper glances at Luca. "Your turn, babe." She starts the timer on her phone and starts off the questions. "Have you ever faked it with me?" Harper jokes with Luca.

"Never." He smirks proudly, and we continue rattling off questions.

"Longest the two of you have gone without sex?" Ashton asks.

Luca snorts. "There was that time I was sick, and she slept in the other room, and we weren't talking. But you should be asking questions about me, not us."

"Do you still hate your father?" I ask. It was no secret that he despised Dante, but now that he's been working for him nearly a year, I'm curious if it's changed.

"Absolutely. But I understand him."

Bristol purses her lips. "Have you ever cheated in hockey?"

"No." His brow pinches.

I can't help but wonder why Bristol would even ask that question. He's the best on the team, why would she think that he'd even need to cheat? And how would that even be possible?

"Cheated on a girl?" Ashton asks.

"Never."

"Are you keeping any secrets from me?" Harper asks.

Luca reaches for the wine bottle and takes a sip.

"What?" her eyes widen. "Seriously, Luca?" She yanks the wine bottle from his grasp, steaming.

He forces a smile, glancing at Bristol. She's watching and he has to be careful not to give too much away. She has no idea of his father's business dealings, that his family is mafia.

"Nothing that matters." He shrugs it off.

"Then tell me what those secrets are." Harper stands, hands on hips, demanding to know what he's keeping from her. "Do you know?" She glares at Ashton and then at me.

I hold my hands up in surrender. "I don't know anything."

Even if I did, it wouldn't be my place to tell Harper.

"You're sleeping in Zeke's room tonight." Harper grumbles and stalks over to the sofa, sitting next to me. She's clearly pissed at her husband.

"Harper." Luca emits a heavy sigh and stands. He strides across the room, holding out a hand for her. "Let's go talk."

"No." She folds her arms across her chest. "We swore there'd be no more secrets." Glaring up at him, she gestures for him to move. "Ashton, it's your turn."

"Are you sure you still want to play?" he asks, glancing from Harper to Luca.

"Yes." Harper purses her lips, and I'm just glad it's not my turn next.

"Fine. Hit me with it." Ashton gestures for her to bring it on.

She starts the timer and the questions start flying out, Harper the first one, and I knew it was coming before she asked it.

"Did you know Luca was keeping secrets from me?"

Ashton nods. "Yes."

Her mouth drops.

I decide it's best steering this game away from destroying Luca and Harper's marriage. I actually like the two of them together.

"How many girls have you knocked up?" I ask.

"Zero. As far as I know."

"How many girls have you slept with?" Bristol asks.

"Don't remember an exact number," Ashton says. "But ballpark, over one hundred and, yes, I'm clean. I've been tested."

"Pet peeve?" I ask, trying to keep things from derailing and turning into a second bloodbath.

"Hockey players not wearing deodorant."

Everyone groans.

"Gross!" Nova glances over her shoulder at Ashton. "When did you first start having feelings for me?"

"The minute your brother told me you were off-limits." Ashton chuckles and holds her tighter against him. "I really started liking you the night of your birthday party. I think I began to see you in a different light. Not just the little sister of my best friend anymore."

The timer buzzes, and I realize we all made it through one round. The tension between Luca and Harper is already terse. Can we survive another round of this game?

"Your turn again," Bristol says cheekily, staring right at me.

"Actually, you went first. If we're playing another round, we rapid fire at you."

She snorts and shrugs. "Go for it."

Harper starts the timer and I just keep thinking this could be a really bad idea. There are so many secrets bottled up that shouldn't get out.

"Do you regret punching me when we were kids?"

"Hardly," Bristol scoffs. "You deserved it." She nudges me on the sofa, a smile on her face, but I can't help but admit it stings.

She doesn't even have a tiny bit of regret for what happened?

"You two knew each other as children?" Harper glances between us.

"Yes," Bristol says before I can answer.

"Will you always hate me?" I ask, needing to know if I'm wasting my time.

"No, I don't know." Bristol rolls her lips together, her brow tightening as she glances at Luca and Ashton, waiting for them to ask something. She's probably hoping they'll offer up some easy questions.

"Are you really interested in Liam, or are you just playing games with him?" Luca asks.

I glance at Luca. Is that what he thinks, or is he trying to protect me like a brother would look out for a sibling?

"I'm not playing games. I don't do that." She shifts uncomfortably, and the timer beeps on Harper's phone.

"Your turn," Bristol says, glaring at me, and I have a definite feeling this game is going from bad to worse.

The timer starts, and Bristol pins me with her stare. "Is your father mafia?"

I reach for the bottle of wine, taking a long swig.

I'm not sure how she knows the answer, but I'm not about to say it aloud. Although, I suppose me drinking is confirmation. I hope that someone else will interject with a less lethal question.

“Do you work for your father?”

“No.” I stare her dead in the eyes, refusing to blink. “My father is in New York City.”

Bristol still isn’t satisfied, asking another question. “Have you ever been arrested?”

“No.”

At least this time, I don’t have anything to hide.

Ashton interrupts with the next question, keeping Bristol from entirely running the game, or maybe he’s just trying to steer away from mafiaesque questions. “Do you prefer to give or receive oral?”

I laugh under my breath. “Are you asking because you’re interested?” I joke. “Give.”

Ashton pretend-coughs. “Liar.”

I glare at him, and he shrugs with a smirk.

“Favorite kink in the bedroom?” Luca asks.

“I like dominating a girl,” I admit.

"Who doesn't?" Ashton glances at Luca. "Am I right?"

Bristol glares at me when she rattles off her next question. "Did you call my father just to piss me off?"

The timer buzzes, but I still answer the question.

"No, I reached out to him because I was worried about you."

And I'm glad my turn is over.

Bristol doesn't meet my stare, she glances away, and the silence is deafening between us. She's stewing, and I want to reach out to her. But I get the distinct feeling if I so much as touch her, she might scream at me.

I have so many questions for Bristol, but it's not her turn. It's Nova's.

How the hell did Bristol know my father is mafia?

Why did she ask if I've ever been arrested?

I suppose I know the answer to one question, is she still mad that I reached out to her father? That's an obvious yes.

Bristol ignores me. Quietly, she gets up and heads past everyone, down the hall, for my bedroom. Bristol doesn't so much as look at me or acknowledge me.

Did I say something wrong?

"Maybe you should go check on her," Harper whispers to me, before resetting the timer for Nova's turn.

Sighing, I stand and head for my bedroom, finding Bristol digging through her overnight bag. Well, she hasn't asked me to take her to the bus station yet.

That's still a good sign.

"Hey." I step into the bedroom. Standing by the door, I size her up, trying to figure out what's going through her head.

Both her mafia and her arrest questions threw me off my game. Then again, I wasn't the nicest, asking if she'd always hate me.

Her answer admittedly stung.

"Hey. I just needed to grab my meds," Bristol says and shows me the container. She walks past me and down the hallway to the kitchen.

I'm right on her heels, following to make sure she's okay.

Silence fills the space between us as I reach into the fridge and grab a bottle of water, and hand it to her.

She opens it, downs the pills along with a swig of water, and finally glances at me, making eye contact. "Thanks."

"Are we ... okay?" I ask. I definitely feel like this game made things worse for us. I'd rather her ask me a hundred sex questions. Even the most embarrassing question is more enjoyable than this awkward shit between us.

Bristol shrugs. "Yeah, I guess so." She can barely make eye contact with me. My hands rest on her hips, pressing her back against the cabinet to stand, before moving one hand to guide her chin to meet my stare.

She exhales loudly, and I swear everyone else in the living room is being quiet so they can eavesdrop on us.

"You can keep playing!" I shout in the vicinity of the living room.

"We're waiting for you guys," Harper shoots back.

"I guess that's our cue." Bristol slips past me, and just as she turns to walk away, I capture her hand in mine. "I need to drop this in my bag before I forget." She reminds me, her pillbox in her other hand.

"I'll do that for you. Go sit, hang out with everyone." I offer her my palm, and she deposits the plastic container in my hand.

"Thanks." Bristol hurries out of the kitchen, and I hear her soft, nervous laughter when she returns to the living room. "Whose turn is it?" she asks.

"Nova's." Harper points at her, seated on Ashton's lap on the floor. Ashton has since climbed onto the beanbag, but Nova has still found her way onto his lap.

I walk past them on the way to my bedroom, drop the plastic container of Bristol's medications into her bag. I try not to snoop, my gaze curious, but I stop myself from causing more drama.

Nope.

None of my business what she brought in her backpack.

All I see are clothes, and I'm not snooping to discover what's on the bottom causing her bag to weigh as much as my hockey gear.

That would have been a great question to ask her: What the hell did she pack in her overnight bag? I just have to hope we can survive another entire round of this dreadful game.

"Hurry up, Liam!" Harper shouts for me to come join them.

I resume my position on the sofa, resting my arm on the back of the couch, my fingers playing with Bristol's dark tendrils as she leans back to get comfy.

My fingers delve from her hair to the back of her neck, and eventually, she scoots closer, her body pressed up against mine.

I listen to the soft breaths of air and try not to get turned on, but the truth is her proximity is enough to make my body respond. She smells amazing; whatever her shampoo or perfume is, it's riveting. All I want to do is drink it in, brush my lips across her neck, and listen to the soft sounds she makes as I tease her.

I shift on the sofa, trying not to let my mind wander to Bristol getting turned on by me, because the next thoughts would be of her *naked*. That's a fantasy for the bedroom, not while I'm seating next to her playing rapid fire questions.

I definitely don't need her asking me why I'm sporting a hard-on midgame.

"Are we playing?" I ask, glancing at Harper, waiting for her to start up the timer for the game.

Nova whispers something into Ashton's ear, and his face reddens. "We're going to head to bed, guys. Have a good night!"

Nova climbs off his weight, and he's got a definite bounce to his step. It's obvious what they intend to do.

"Keep the noise level down," Luca growls at them. "Zeke is sleeping."

Right, like he and Harper ever keep it down. The two of them don't know how to have quiet sex. There have been nights that I had to put on my noise cancelling headphones to keep from hearing the two of them, and their room is closer to Zeke's than it is to mine.

That kid is lucky he can sleep through anything.

"Harper." Luca gestures for her to join him on the love seat.

She tosses her middle finger up at him. It's clear she's still pissed. I don't want to meddle, and as much as I hate seeing them fight, I get the feeling that they will find their way back to each other. They always do.

Luca stands and strolls across the room. Growling, he grabs Harper, lifts her up, puts her over his shoulder, and carries her into his bedroom.

"Put me down!" Harper squeals, pounding his ass with her closed fists as she fights him the entire way.

SEVENTEEN

HARPER

“How dare you!” I seethe.

Luca plants my feet firmly on the ground in our bedroom, the door kicked shut behind him.

He forces a smile, there’s no anger in his stance, and I suspect that he has little remorse as well.

“Is this about the game?” Luca asks.

“It’s about you keeping secrets from me, after you explicitly promised that you wouldn’t do that!” I stand toe-to-toe with him.

Luca is so much taller that he towers above me. But

I'm not the least bit intimidated by him. I jab my finger into his chest.

"You lied to me!"

He grabs my hand, intertwining our fingers, trying to disarm me; although my only weapon is my finger. It's not like I'm actually going to cause him any harm.

"I kept things from you, yes, but you can't expect me to tell you everything that Dante has me working on."

My mouth drops. "This isn't about Dante. It's about you and me," I growl, and he moves to sit at the edge of the mattress, letting me be the one towering over him.

He reaches for my hips, keeping me close, his touch warm and inviting, but I shove his hands away.

"You can't use sex to get out of this argument."

Luca quirks a grin. "Can't I?" He raises an eyebrow and tugs off his shirt, throwing it at me.

"You're an asshole sometimes." I shove him onto his back, straddling his waist. "I ought to fucking tease you until you explode."

"Who's the one being a brat now?" He smiles up at me, like he just won this round.

The hell he didn't.

I move my hips against his, teasing him, watching his eyes shut mercilessly as he craves the pleasure building up between us.

"We're not having sex tonight," I snap.

"Tell that to your hips." His voice is raspy and his eyes have darkened as he runs his fingers over the hem of my shirt, his fingers slipping under the material, grazing bare flesh.

His touch is electrifying, but I force down the building desire within me.

"Tell me everything you know about that guy with the tattoo. The one who is after my son!" I slam Luca's hands down against the bed, keeping him from turning this moment sexual, as I have him pinned down under my weight.

"He's Massimo's son. I called Dante earlier, and it looks like he's taken over the family business of the DeLuca's and he's calling the shots. He wants Zeke because we killed his father."

"We?" I stare down at Luca, my grip loosening only slightly.

"I did it. I killed him. It was all me." He stares up at me, into my soul, and I can't tell if he's taking the blame for Dante, or he quite literally pulled the trigger and murdered a man.

I roll off his body, needing space, air to breathe, and I climb off the bed.

"Where are you going, Harper?" There's worry in his voice and for good reason.

He just told me he murdered a man!

"This is revenge, some sort of vengeance," I say, trying to gather all the facts even though Luca keeps hiding truths from me. "He wants Zeke as some sort of sick payback."

Breathing heavily, Luca sits up and nods. "I believe so, but you don't have to worry. We have surveillance around the house, there's always one of us with you. Tomorrow, I'm taking you to the shooting range and signing you up for self-defense classes in the evening."

I certainly hadn't noticed having a personal bodyguard every time I left the house. But now that I think back, I can't remember the last time that I was alone. "What?"

He pauses for a moment, trying to ascertain my question.

"There are cameras outside the property. We've got Dante's men watching over the house, and I've been talking with him about—"

"No." I cut him off before he can tell me what he's been discussing with Dante.

That man despises me.

"No, what?" Luca shakes his head, meeting my stare.

"I don't want Dante's help. He's the reason for this mess. He's the reason my son's life is in danger!"

Luca runs a hand through his hair. He's trying to remain calm, I can see the inner turmoil cross his face. "He just wants to help."

"I don't want his help," I grit between clenched teeth. "I blame him."

"Fine. Blame him all you want, but he's the reason we're all living under this roof, here to protect you."

I'm taken aback by his remark. That doesn't sound right. It certainly doesn't sound like Dante.

"Excuse me?"

Luca glances away.

Silence.

"Don't you dare hold back now!" I storm across the room, my hand gripping his arm, pleading with him for the truth. "Tell me everything, Luca!"

"The scholarships, at least the hockey ones, were all orchestrated by my father. It was his way to ensure my allegiance and that I'd join the family business after college."

"You're fucking kidding me." I drop my hold on his arm.

"Tell me about it," he grumbles. "My future, laid out for me without my consent." He stands, rage tearing through him, his jaw clenches, his fists tightening at his sides as he struggles to keep his composure. Each word that leaves his mouth is edged with frustration and helplessness, a storm threatening to break at any moment.

"Well, tell him no. Don't follow in his footsteps. Leave him, quit. Walk away. He doesn't own you and he can't lay a finger on Zeke. We won't let him."

Luca lets out a bitter laugh, the sound jagged and hallow. "I can't walk away." His words send a shiver down my spine. The darkness flows so easily out of him that it startles me.

I'm not afraid of him. His father, on the other hand, Dante frightens me. "What the hell, Luca? Why not?" I ask, wanting to know what's stopping him. "You can apply for financial aid. If it's your father's money hanging over you—"

"It's not his money," he growls and glances down at the floor, the heaviness hanging over him like a storm cloud.

Luca avoids my stare.

He won't look at me, the guilt weighing heavily on him.

My heart hammers like a pounding, steady rain. I'd

failed to see it earlier, or perhaps I wanted to ignore it.

"You murdered a man," I whisper, remembering what he'd told me minutes earlier.

His tongue darts out, and he chances a glance up at me. "Are you scared yet?"

EIGHTEEN

LIAM

There's clearly a lot of arguing happening between Luca and Harper. The last thing I want is for Bristol to catch wind of what they're fighting about.

"How about we head to bed?" I ask, offering her my hand. I lead her to the bedroom and let her get dressed in her pajamas while I close up for the night.

I shut off the lights and make sure the house is secure before joining Bristol in my bedroom.

I give a soft knock on my door.

"Come in," she answers.

I step into the room that I've been in hundreds of times, but this time it feels different.

The air is charged, heated.

It's Bristol's presence, no doubt, that makes it feel that way.

She's seated on my mattress, her legs buried under the covers. She nervously chews her bottom lip, and I strip down to my boxers.

Her nervousness exudes off and straight onto me.

My stomach roils, and I force a smile. "We're just going to sleep. Okay?"

Relief floods her face. "Okay. Can we talk, though, or is that off-limits?"

Smiling, I pull back the covers and stretch out, joining her in my bed.

I never thought I'd see the day that Bristol Greyson is in my bed with me. Maybe as a cruel joke, but not because she likes me.

She does like me, doesn't she?

Worry starts edging its way into my head.

Bristol scoots down farther on the mattress, coming to lie on her side, staring at me. "You look like you've seen a ghost," she whispers.

"Maybe I have." I reach for the bedside lamp and shut it off, basking the room in darkness. "Or maybe I just never expected to find you in my bed."

She chuckles softly and wraps her arms around my waist, instantly curling into me.

It's a nice feeling, her body cocooned to mine. I pull her closer, tighter, resting my chin on the top of her head.

"Hey, don't do that." She wiggles free and my cock responds to her lower body movements.

Down, boy.

Now is not the time for *that*.

I mean, yes, we're in bed together, but she doesn't seem ready, and that's a hard no for me.

I should consider driving her home, but it's late, and she hasn't asked to leave.

I take that as a sign that she wants to stay, or maybe it's just me feeling foolishly hopeful.

She rests her head on her pillow, her eyes sparkling in the darkness as I stare at her, unable to look away.

"Can we talk about that game earlier?" I ask.

Bristol shifts, but I can't tell if she's shrugging or just getting comfortable. The bed dips slightly, and then she answers, "Maybe. What do you want to talk about, Liam?"

"Why did you ask me if my father is mafia?"

I shouldn't even bring it up. I drank to avoid the question, but now I'm being completely reckless and mentioning it again.

I need to know where she's getting her information. Is there a leak in his organization? It shouldn't be common knowledge that he runs the New York City mafia. He tries to keep a low profile; at least, I think he does.

We don't talk business.

Unlike Luca and Ashton, my father isn't preparing me to run his empire.

"He is mafia, isn't he?" Bristol asks.

I let silence be my answer.

"Okay," Bristol sighs. "What if I told you I know, without a doubt, that he runs the mafia in New York City and—"

"Do you have evidence?"

"Me? Of course not. It's just, I interned for the summer at Eagle Tactical, and I saw—"

"What did you see?" I sit up in bed, my heart racing.

"There were files, pages on your family, my family. It's quite complicated. For a minute, I thought we might have been related."

I can't help but raise an eyebrow as I stare down at her.

She's joking, right?

"I had the same expression," Bristol says. The smile softens on her face. "It's okay. We're not related, but the files—"

"What files?" I growl.

"The ones they have on everyone. They run background checks for like every local business in town. They also do private investigative work. What's your problem?" she asks, realizing I'm not lying back down and going to sleep.

All she's done is worked me up into a frenzy.

"My father is in those files? Am *I* in those files?"

"You're mentioned, but it's nothing bad. Just that you're his son. What's the big deal?" Bristol asks.

She has no idea the man Antonio is and what he's capable of. If he got wind that there was anything on him, so much as a file with his name on it, he'd burn that place to the ground and everyone along with it.

"Stay away from anything involving my father," I growl at her.

"Obviously," Bristol says, forcing a smile. "I don't plan on working for the mafia." She laughs and runs her hand along my arm and down to my hand.

Her touch is soothing, but I still feel pent-up frustration jumping through my veins, making it impossible to lie down and fall asleep.

"I didn't ask you that to stress you out or embarrass you in front of your friends," Bristol says.

I shuffle back down on the mattress, lying on my side, staring at her. "Why did you ask me about it?"

"I wanted to know if you knew he was mafia. Seems like you do."

"It'd be impossible not to know," I whisper. "I'd have to be dumb. Doesn't mean I'm rolling over on him. I have nothing. No evidence. Never saw him commit a crime. I'd make a terrible witness on the stand, and as far as I know, he's just a very astute businessman."

"Uh-huh, sure." Bristol isn't convinced, but I don't need to convince her. I just need her to leave it well enough alone. "Are you mad at me for asking?"

I exhale a heavy sigh. "No," I say and pull her closer. "I'm not mad. I was just surprised."

"Do you think your friends are going to be afraid of you, now that they know your father is mafia?"

I'm grateful for the darkness, that she can't read all the features on my face like she could if we were under lamplight. "I think they'll be okay."

Bristol shrugs. "If I found out my roommate's father was mafia, I'd be a little freaked out."

"What about if your boyfriend's father were mafia?" I ask. At least I don't have to worry about her making a colossal fuck up like Harper did the first time she met his parents.

Bristol slides a leg between mine, hooking herself around me. It's a small but possessive gesture. "Are you asking me to be your girlfriend?"

"Only if you'll say yes."

"Absolutely."

I pull her atop me, my hands at her lower back as I drink her scent in.

"Are you sure we won't kill each other?" She laughs, brushing her lips over mine in a tentative kiss.

"That's a promise I can't make," I confess. We tend to run hot and cold, except now, I suspect things are going to get hell of a lot spicier between us.

NINETEEN

HARPER

I should be afraid of Luca. He murdered a man, but I know it was to protect the family, *my family*.

I'm trying to accept that I can't know everything he's involved in, but that doesn't make it any easier.

After class, I pick up Zeke, and we grab dinner at the dining hall before bringing him home. Nova accompanies me through all of it, and I wonder how much is want and how much is playing bodyguard because the guys are at practice and she's been told to babysit me.

Is she working for Dante now, too?

Zeke doesn't want to be carried home, so I keep a close eye on him as we walk along the sidewalk, making sure that he doesn't get too far ahead.

It does help to have another set of eyes keeping lookout.

I feel overly paranoid lately, but after the incident at the daycare, how could I not?

The clouds are rolling in fast, and while it's warm today, the air is suddenly chilled. We head inside the house and Nova locks the doors, setting the security alarm. We've been more diligent about turning it on when we're home. I'll admit, I'm one of the worst when it came to setting the alarm, always forgetting about it, because I had felt safe.

Nova drops the mail on the kitchen table and sorts through it. "Shit. Ashton got a letter from the Student Conduct Office. That can't be good."

"Isn't that for disciplinary measures? Ashton hasn't done anything. Did something happen during a game or after?" The guys are always fighting during a hockey game, but that wouldn't result in any type of letter from the student conduct office, would it?

Nova exhales a heavy sigh. "No, I think I know what it's about."

"What?" I glance up at her, concerned.

"The teaching assistant in our Criminology class said some things that were inappropriate. I thought I took care of it, but Ashton had bruised knuckles and the following session in class, the teaching assistant had a bruised jaw. I was hoping I was wrong about those two."

Grimacing, I glance at the enclosed envelope. It's impossible to read through the thick packet, the paper folded in thirds.

"Maybe it's something else?" I'm trying to be hopeful, but if Ashton assaulted a teaching assistant, then it's grounds for expulsion.

I get Zeke ready for bed, dressing him in his pajamas and reading him a story before tucking him in for the night.

The wind picks up, and I can hear thunder rumbling off in the distance.

Zeke is tired and crabby, and before the story is finished, he's already fallen asleep.

I give him a kiss goodnight and quietly close the door behind me.

As I stand in the hallway, the sound of breaking glass shattering and crunching under footsteps sends a shiver down my spine.

Did someone just break a window?

The alarm is eerily silent.

I want to be wrong.

The wind roars and is louder than before.

Could the storm have blown out a window?

Nova jumps up from the sofa, her eyes wide, and we exchange a look of apprehension.

She heard it, too—the sound unmistakable.

Fear jolts through my veins. "Go get Zeke," I order her as I hurry the three feet to the hall closet and retrieve the gun hidden on the top shelf in the back.

Hands trembling, the gun is already loaded, and I cock off the safety, prepared to use it if absolutely necessary. I'm grateful that just last week, for the first time, Ashton and Luca took me to the shooting range.

I'm not a great shot from a distance, but up close, I can at least hit the target in the chest, which is all I need.

I'm not going for a sniper medal. I just need to be able to protect my son and my family.

Footsteps.

It's definitely not just a storm.

The footsteps are heavy, like boots trudging through mud, careful, precise, quiet, but not silent enough.

Nova opens the bedroom door to Zeke's room. The man with the snake tattoo appears, holding my sleeping son over one shoulder, and a gun in his other hand.

"Harper," Nova's voice catches in her throat.

Zeke hasn't stirred, and an evil smile sneaks across the tattooed man's face. "I should thank your husband for murdering my father, Massimo, but I won't." He flashes a toothless grin and raises his gun at me. "But I am taking the child with me."

"Hand over my son," I growl, gun poised at the tattooed man. I can't aim for the center of his chest without risking hitting Zeke. There's too much distance between us.

A week at the shooting range is barely enough time to feel confident in my ability to shoot the assailant and not hurt my boy.

"The way I see it, the Riccis released all those girls, you owe me. The boy will be taken as collateral, and I won't harm a hair on his head, you have my word unless you or the Riccis come after me or my enterprise."

I step closer to the madman, my gun poised, my hand slightly trembling, but I pray he doesn't notice. "You'll need nothing when you're dead."

"On the contrary, you won't shoot me. Not while I have your little boy in my arms. You're too weak to pull the trigger, too complacent. You'll follow my orders if you and your friend want to live." His gun is poised on me, not Zeke, which is my only advantage.

My life is nothing without Zeke.

I close the distance between us, the gap mere inches, the barrel of my gun almost touching his chest.

"You won't," he smirks, convinced I don't have it in me to pull the trigger.

He's wrong.

He has to be, because I won't let anyone take my son from me.

The deafening roar of thunder outside almost drowns out the sharp crack of my gunshot. For a split second, time stands still.

Two shots fire from the assailant's gun, but I feel nothing.

Only fear.

The smell of burnt gunpowder fills the air as the tattooed man staggers backward, a crimson stain blooming across his chest.

My heart slams wildly against my ribcage. I catch a glimpse of Zeke's terrified face, his small body shaking as he's startled awake, caught between confusion and terror.

His scream matches the intensity of the rain as it lashes against the windows, the storm raging as fiercely inside as out.

Nova is right beside me, her voice cuts through the tension, steady yet urgent. "Come here," she says, grabbing Zeke, sheltering him from the brutality, covering his eyes as she ushers him away from the violence, away from me.

I stand rooted, my mind reeling, the weight of my actions pressing heavily on my shoulders as I watch the man collapse.

I had no choice.

Zeke is safe, but the guilt of not being able to protect him already claws at my conscience.

I kick the gun away from the man's reach as he gasps hard for breath.

Lightning crackles across the sky, flashing through the windows.

Another boom of thunder rings overhead.

"Who sent you?" I position the gun at the assailant's forehead, demanding answers.

He coughs and chokes, his fingers itching for the trigger, but the gun isn't within his grasp. "No one. I run the damn mafia!"

"Not anymore." I stare down at him and pull the trigger one last time, ensuring his demise.

"No one threatens my son."

TWENTY

NOVA

I shield Zeke from the horror of what he just witnessed, but the screams and tears don't stop. He woke up in the arms of a madman holding a gun, threatening his mother.

The kid will have nightmares for life, just like Luca. Just like me.

But Zeke didn't lose his mother.

Thankfully, she wasn't shot.

I wasn't as lucky.

My mother was murdered in daylight, outside, on a crisp autumn morning.

When I close my eyes, I can still see it, smell the gunpowder, hear the gunshots.

I'd been playing outside in the yard, jumping in piles of colorful leaves when armed, masked men stormed through the gates.

Mom had been having coffee and breakfast outside on the veranda when they shot her from behind. She didn't even see them coming.

My nanny hid me in the bushes, told me we were playing hide and seek and not to come out, no matter what. She protected me before she faced the masked men and was brutally murdered in cold blood.

After that, I was mute for years. I refused to speak to anyone, afraid what might happen if I got too close to someone.

I don't want that fear for Zeke.

I carry him out of the hallway into the living room, trying desperately to comfort him, but he is inconsolable.

"We have to call the cops," Harper says, walking into the living room, the gun still in her hand.

That's the worst idea. I can't let her do that. "No. Stop. Think about what you're saying."

"It was self-defense!" Harper raises her voice and winces when Zeke begins howling even louder.

"You and I know that, but the police—we can't trust them." Does she not realize the cops aren't on our side?

"You're just saying that because your father is mafia. We can trust the police," Harper says and reaches for her phone.

I snatch it out of her hand.

"Promise me, not until we talk to Luca and Ashton." I don't want her making things worse than they already are.

"I can't get ahold of him right now. They're at practice. I can't just show up, either, I'm covered in blood!" Harper glances at her appearance.

"Shower. Change," I reason with her.

"But there's evidence. *I'm covered in evidence*. I can't —" She shakes her head. "Won't the cops have heard the gunshots?"

I shrug. I'm not sure if anyone would have reported the gunfire. They could just as easily believe it to be from the thunderstorm if we're lucky.

I keep cuddling Zeke, who has a bit of blood dried to his cheeks from the splatter, and I take him into the kitchen to wipe away the remnants.

"What are you doing?" Harper is right on my heel, following my every move.

"Cleaning your son." I gape at her, the gun still in her hand. "Put that thing away before you accidentally discharge it."

She stalks off while I run the sink, sit Zeke at the edge of the counter and dip the kitchen towel under the lukewarm water. I wipe at his rosy cheeks, which are both red from crying and from dried blood. He has a little in his hair, too, which I try to wipe clean.

"But that's evidence," Harper pleads with me, her eyes red-rimmed, and I realize she's holding on to her sanity by a thread.

I understand her rationale, her reasoning for wanting to call the police, she's trying to justify what she's done—to herself, maybe even to us.

Sighing, I glance at her for a brief moment. "Text Luca." I try to be the voice of reason. I offer her back her phone. "Don't call him and don't say anything incriminating." I don't trust that she can keep herself together if she's on the phone. She's about ready to break, I can see it in the tremor in her hands, the fluctuation in her breathing, and the slight crack in her voice.

"So, I shouldn't tell him I just killed the man who tried abducting my son?" Harper mocks, her brow furrowed, and I see past her dark humor, for the fresh pain she's harboring.

"Not funny, Harper."

With her back to me, I text my father.

Trouble.

He doesn't even respond via text; immediately, he calls me on the encrypted line.

"What the hell is going on?" Dad's always right to the point. I suppose he's used to dealing with messes, they're just not usually mine.

"There was a break-in this evening. Some guy with a snake tattoo went after Zeke." I'm hesitant to give any more specifics, encrypted or not, I have my own worries.

"The child?" Dad asks. Two words. He wants to know if he's been taken or harmed.

"Fine. The assailant has been stopped but—"

"Say no more," he cuts me off before I can tell him there's some cleaning up to do.

Harper spins around when she realizes I'm on the phone. "Who the hell are you talking to?"

"My father," I say.

"I can't call the cops, but you can call your dad, the mafia?" Harper throws her arms up into the air. "I didn't do anything wrong. It was self-defense. Why do you have to involve *them?*"

TWENTY-ONE

LUCA

When we finish practice, I notice the barrage of texts on my phone coming from Harper.

"Ashton, did you get any messages?" I ask, wondering what the hell is going on, but already, my stomach is in knots.

Harper wouldn't be sending me frantic texts unless something bad happened.

Harper: Get home now!

Harper: Luca, I need you.

Harper: Nova called her father.

Shit.

If it's as bad as I suspect, texting and calling will leave behind evidence. I refrain from reaching out to Harper. I'll be home soon. Five more minutes won't make any difference.

"Yeah," Ashton grumbles. We rush to get dressed from our practice attire. Thankfully, we already showered, or I'd be skipping it.

The three of us hurry out of the locker room and head back to the house.

There's been zero communication from Dante or Moreno. But if Nova reached out to her old man, then it's possible they're now involved in whatever is happening at home.

Fear threatens my senses as I near the house, worried what I might find.

Lightning flashes overhead as the storm refuses to ease its severe hold over the town. The rain has slowed, but the wind is whipping around. Lightning illuminates the night sky. Thunder cracks overhead with a sharp bang.

There are no police cars.

No ambulances.

Minus the storm, everything is quiet.

Dark.

Except for the faint light glowing from inside the house behind the closed curtains, nothing looks out of the ordinary, but I *feel* it.

As we approach the house, Zeke's screams reach the porch—he sounds inconsolable. I unlock the front door, but I don't see anyone yet.

"Harper? What's going on? Is everyone okay?" I'm afraid for my wife, my son, my sister—for all three of them.

Harper comes barreling toward me, her eyes glassy and red, her hands trembling, covered in blood.

I embrace her, glancing her over quickly, making sure she isn't injured or bleeding.

"Are you okay? Whose blood is that?"

Nova is cradling my son, trying to offer him comfort, but it doesn't seem to help.

They're all alive.

I almost have time to breathe a sigh of relief, but the blood concerns me greatly.

"What the hell happened?"

Wordlessly, Harper nods. Her hands tremble, and I realize her entire body is shaking.

I try to inspect her as quickly as I can, looking for injuries. "The blood, Harper. Whose is it?" I try again, this time more agitated that she can't focus.

She's probably in shock from whatever transpired, but I don't like being kept waiting or in the dark.

"His—" Harper gestures to the hallway behind her, and there's a trail of blood seeping into the carpet.

I glance past her, take a side-step, and I can see the body, the man crumpled on the floor.

"He's dead," Nova says, confirming the question I haven't yet asked.

"He broke into Zeke's bedroom and was kidnapping my son. I had to stop him. It was self-defense."

"*Our* son," I correct her, pulling her against me. "How did you shoot him?"

"With a gun."

I pull back, surprised. Did she really just answer with a smartass remark?

The look on her face tells me she's disassociating. Her mind is far from her body, probably reliving the trauma over and over again.

My jaw clenches. I hate that I wasn't there to protect her. My hands are on her cheeks as I try to get her to make eye contact with me.

"The weapon, Harper. What gun did you use?" I grind out.

"The one in the hall closet."

Shit.

We had a gun in our bedroom closet, locked and stored securely, which was intended to be used in the event of a break-in or attack.

She wasn't supposed to use the gun in the hall closet.

In fact, she wasn't even supposed to know about it, but when she found it putting linens away, I didn't want to worry her. I made up the excuse that it was solely to be used for emergencies, because, quite frankly, that gun could land my ass in prison. I made it abundantly clear it was not to be used at the shooting range.

The gun needed to disappear. Why the hell hadn't Ashton gotten rid of the evidence?

It was *his* gun that I used to shoot and kill Massimo.

Wincing, I curse and glance her over. This evening just went from bad to worse. "Get showered and dressed. You need clean clothes. We need to burn all of the evidence."

"Burn it?" Harper repeats, her brow pinched. "Why?" Slowly, she's coming back, like she's been sinking at the bottom of a pool and is finally breaking the surface, coming up for air.

Ashton and Liam help Nova with Zeke, trying to settle him down until I finally offer a hand.

But Zeke doesn't want me.

I wrestle him from Nova and cuddle him, trying to calm him down, offering him kisses and hugs, even grabbing a grape popsicle from the freezer, hoping to distract him with his favorite flavor.

The tears are now silent but keep flowing, and

Harper can't seem to look at him and can barely look at me.

I carry Zeke closer to Harper, but stand so that the dead body isn't in Zeke's line of sight. Zeke slowly licks his popsicle, his eyes red and splotchy as he sniffles. A few more tears streak down his cheeks.

I rest my forehead against Harper's. "What's going through your head?" It's just the three of us, Harper, Zeke, and me.

Nova is relaying everything that happened to Ashton and Liam in the living room, giving them the full details of the assailant and what Harper had to do.

"I shot him in self-defense." Harper's answer reaches not only my ears, but Liam and Ashton's as well.

"I believe you," I say, nodding. "But we can't go to the police. Not if you used that gun." I nod toward the weapon on the floor.

"Why not?" Her glassy eyes meet my stare.

"Because that same gun was used to kill Massimo DeLuca. If you go to the police and turn in that weapon, you'll be sending me to prison for life. My DNA is all over the murder weapon."

Her gaze lowers as she turns and stares at his lifeless body on the floor. How the hell are we going to lug him out, dispose of him, and get rid of all the evidence?

"I'd never want to hurt you," she whispers.

"Good, then you know that we can't go to the police."

She shakes her head, her brow tightening as her jaw trembles and she's fighting back tears. "No." There's desperation in her tone, fear, and something else.

"They'll lock me away, Harper. If they connect the dots and realize that weapon has been used in a previous killing—"

"I wouldn't do that. I won't." Harper swallows, a frown etched across her face. "You don't trust me."

"I trust you, it's why I told you the truth about Massimo." I hadn't wanted to tell her, and it had only been days ago that I'd fully come clean about it, but the truth was still in her hands to do with as she sees fit.

She could have me arrested and locked up for murder.

Her brow is tight, and she grabs my arm, imploring me with that look of utter determination. “I won’t risk your life, Luca, not after everything you’ve done for me.”

I slide my hand into hers, giving it a reaffirming squeeze. We’re in this together.

“Tell me what I have to do,” she says.

A prominent knock taps roughly against the front door.

Her eyes widen and she glances at the deceased’s body on the floor.

“Go shower,” I tell her, pointing at the bathroom.

She’ll have to walk past the dead body, but she needs to rid herself of the evidence, and right now, she’s still caked in blood.

Wordlessly, she nods and heads to the bathroom, her eyes focusing on the dead body on the floor.

Another firm knock on the door.

I can’t hear who is on the other end, but I want Harper out of those bloody clothes. She’s not going to help anyone if she answers the door covered in gore.

Zeke sniffles and takes another lick of his popsicle. His face is red, rosy, and I try and cheer him up while his mom showers.

Another, more persistent knock, and whoever is at the front door isn't going away.

"It's too soon to be my dad," Nova says, glancing at her phone.

"Open up, Evergreen University Police!"

To Be Continued.

SHOP SIGNED AND EXCLUSIVE EDITIONS

THANK you so much for reading Between Steel and Secrets. I hope you enjoyed the novel. Be sure to sign up for my newsletter for up-to-date new release details, sales, early release news, and more!

If you love signed paperbacks, special edition books, or discounted book bundles be sure to check out my online bookshop: https://shopwillowfox.com

ABOUT THE AUTHOR

Willow Fox has written in multiple genres. She's written everything from young adult dystopian to spicy RomCom novels. Her books have been translated into five languages and sold across the world.

Whether Willow is writing romance or sitting outside by the bonfire reading a good book, she loves the magic of the written word.

Follow her on any of her social media sites or through her newsletter!

Willow also writes kinky romance books under the pen name Allison West.

Visit her website at:

shopwillowfox.com

ALSO BY WILLOW FOX

Eagle Tactical Series

Expose: Jaxson

Stealth: Mason

Conceal: Lincoln

Covert: Jayden

Truce: Declan

Mafia Marriages

Secret Vow

Captive Vow

Savage Vow

Unwilling Vow

Ruthless Vow

Bratva Brothers

Brutal Boss

Wicked Boss

Possessive Boss

Obsessive Boss

Dangerous Boss

Bossy Single Dad Series

Billionaire Grump

Mountain Grump

Bachelor Grump

Ice Dragons Hockey Romance

Faking it with the Billionaire

Daring the Hockey Player

Arresting the Hockey Player

Crimson Ice

Between Blades and Blood

Between Ice and Oaths

Between Fire and Frost

Between Sin and Silence

Between Steel and Secrets

Between Storms and Scars

Want more kinky romance? I also write under the pen name Allison West.

Gem Apocalypse Series

Emerald Rebellion

Amber Voyeur

Sapphire Sacrifice

Scarlet Assassin

Crimson Crown

Royally Claimed Series

Palace Secrets

Maiden Claimed

Grave Misfortune

Academy of Littles

Little Etta

Little Gigi

Little Eliza

Reforming the Rebellious

Little Lizzie's Reform (Little Lizzie)

Little Prim and Proper (Little Kat)

Virtue and Vice

A Proper Punishment (Little Lena)

Little Brides (Little Clara)

Dowries and Deception

Delia's Debt (Little Delia)

Decoy Bride (Little Vera)

Jessie's Secret

Violet's Penance

Piper's Escape

Fiery Luna

Little Jade

Little Alice

Little Love Bundle/Western Daddies

Little Samantha

Little Lexa

Little Autumn

Little Rosie

Prefer a sweeter romance with action and adventure? Check out these titles under the name Ruth Silver.

Aberrant Series

Love Forbidden

Secrets Forbidden

Magic Forbidden

Escape Forbidden

Refuge Forbidden

Nightblood

Royal Reaper

Stolen Art

www.ingramcontent.com/pod-product-compliance
Lightning Source LLC
La Vergne TN
LVHW100511110826
845146LV00002B/598

* 9 7 9 8 8 8 6 3 7 3 2 0 2 *